Everything I Know About You

BELiNDA HOLLYER

ORCHARD BOOKS

ORCHARD BOOKS
338 Euston Road, London NW1 3BH
Orchard Books Australia
Level 17/207 Kent Street, Sydney, NSW 2000

ISBN 978 1 84616 766 9

A paperback original
First published in 2008

Text © Belinda Hollyer 2008
The 7-line quotation on page 44 is from 'A Spell for Sleeping' by Alistair
Reid, used by kind permission of the author.

10 9 8 7 6 5 4 3 2 1

Printed and bound by CPI Cox & Wyman, Reading, Berkshire RG1 8EX

A CIP catalogue record for this book is available from the British Library.

The paper used in this paperback are natural recyclable products made from
wood grown in sustainable forests. The manufacturing processes conform to
the environmental regulations of the country of origin.

Orchard Books is a division of Hachette Children's Books,
an Hachette Livre UK company.

www.hachettelivre.co.uk

1

Dad says I look like Mum when I put my hair in a ponytail on top of my head, but my little brother Eric just thinks I look like a pony. And if I didn't have a story to tell you that has nothing much to do with hair and nothing at all to do with ponies I could leave it at that, and you'd still know the most important things about both of them: that Dad likes remembering Mum, and that Eric likes using his imagination.

Eric loves it when I go along with him on the pony idea, and toss my head and whinny and gallop around. He does it too, and we prance through the flat together like wild horses, and sometimes we recite part of a poem that Mum used to say to me. It goes like this:

A thousand horse, the wild, the free
Like waves that follow o'er the sea,
Came thickly thundering on...

Mum loved poems. We even used to make them up together off the top of our heads. She'd turn it into a game; she'd say, 'Close your eyes, Lizzie love, and tell me what you see.'

And I'd think of something, like, say, fishes. And then if it was bedtime, or if she wanted to soothe me down, she'd tell me a fishy story or recite a fishy poem. Mum knew a poem to go with almost anything because she could remember hundreds of them off by heart. For fishes, just as one example, she'd start with an old nursery rhyme that goes like this:

'Where are you going and what do you wish?'
The old moon asked the three.
'We have come to fish for the herring fish
That live in this beautiful sea;
Nets of silver and gold have we!'
Said Wynken,
Blynken,
And Nod.

But more often she'd make up the first line of

a poem about fishes, and I'd do the next line, and we'd go on taking turns until we'd finished it. If the poem turned out well we'd write it down and draw a picture for it. I've got one of the best fish poems we ever did together up on my bedroom wall. Dad put it in a clip frame for me when we moved here, after Mum died.

> *Silvery shining spangled fishes*
> *glinting in the river*
> *like flickers of light.*
> *A reedy trail of bubbles*
> *then – gone again.*

I'm still proud of that one, even now that I write fairly good poems by myself. Well, I think they're OK, anyway. I don't show them to other people, so I don't know what anyone else's opinion would be.

I try to remember everything Mum did with me, and with Eric when he was a baby, because I don't want to lose anything I know about her. Sometimes I worry about remembering what she looked like, though, because trying doesn't always work. Mostly I can picture her easily in my head. I can even make her move around and talk to me, like there's a camcorder rolling in my brain. But other times I can't remember how she looked at all, like the camcorder's stuck or the battery's run down. That's scary; I think I'm losing her all over again. We have photos of Mum all over our flat, but I test myself on remembering the Mum who *isn't* in the photos, because they don't show her doing every single thing I ever knew. And mostly I can fill in other memories, but other times I can only see Photo Mum.

Photo Mum's still better than no memory at all, though, and that's what Eric has. Eric was only two when Mum died; it's absolutely not his fault that he doesn't remember her. He says he does but I don't see how he can, and I think what's happened is that he's made up memories from all our stories and photos. But like Dad says, that's the best Eric can do, and as long as we keep talking about Mum and telling him stories about her, that'll give him something true to go on.

Dad and I made Eric a memory box after she died. We put things in it we thought he'd like to have – stuff that was important to Mum, plus some things about Mum and Eric together. He was too little for it then but he likes it now – he keeps it on the chest of drawers in his bedroom. After we'd made it I had second thoughts. I got worried that it looked too girly for him, because I'd covered the box with pale-pink paper that had swirly pink lines all over it. But he doesn't seem to mind – he's never complained, anyway. He often talks to the box and tells it about his day, and he makes up stories for it, like I do for him and like Mum did for me. He invents good stories, I have to say.

Dad says Eric runs on ninety-nine per cent imagination and one per cent reality. And it's true that Eric doesn't just want to talk about dinosaurs or dragons or Spiderman: he actually wants to *be* them. When he invents a game, he throws himself into it with his whole heart. To tell you the truth, I still enjoy making up games with him even though I've been twelve for months now, and Eric's only just seven. But even if I didn't enjoy them I'd still want to play with him like Mum played with me. I sort of owe it to him.

Eric's imagination has been stuck on dragons for a while now. Dad says he's turned into a one-boy dragon theme park, but Eric just says that dragons are his best thing ever. He makes dragon heads to wear out of paper carrier bags from shops – everyone we know in our block of flats saves the big ones for him. Eric doesn't actually make the heads by himself; I have to help because he's so impatient and wants things to be right the absolute first second he tries to do them. When that doesn't happen he gets majorly frustrated and upset, and if you don't want things to end badly, you lend a hand.

Our au pair, Bex, she's great at helping with Eric's projects, too. It was Bex who invented the idea of using spare buttons to make dragon scales, and in fact she's very good at lots of crafty things. She taught me to do something that she calls French knitting, but Bex is Australian, so I call it Aussie knitting when I show other people how to do it. I've got lots of girls in my year keen on it, plus even one of the boys!

You start off with an old cotton reel and stick nails around one end, or if you can't find a wooden cotton reel you can buy a special kit with the nails already in place. And then you weave wool around the nails in a kind of figure-of-eight and lift the wool over the pins... Well, it's hard to explain in words what you do, but it's easy to show someone. Anyway, all that winding and lifting makes a round tube of knitting come out the other end and you can make the tube as long as you like. Then you can turn it into fake plaits for your hair, or sew it around the hem of a jumper or the edge of a beret, or fold and knot it into a flower and pin it on your jacket. You can even curl it up flat like a snake and make table mats for presents. Or tie bows of it onto a kite's tail. Or, in Eric's particular case, you can safety-pin it to the back of your T-shirt for a dragon's tail.

When Eric does his full-on fire-breathing dragon thing he puts on a dragon head and waves his knitted tail around with one hand, while he roars and stalks and pounces. Frankly, I'd rather be the dragon, who's always the star of his games and gets all the action, instead of being the princess, who's only there because the dragon wants to eat her. It's boring always having to be tied to a rock, but like I said, I'd rather play with Eric than not. And luckily, Bex doesn't mind taking turns at being the princess. She has a terrific shrieking scream she does when the dragon arrives roaring and waving his tail. Dad says the first time he heard it his heart almost stopped with fright because he thought something terrible had happened to us, but it was only Bex's ace acting.

She's a very good sport, Bex, and she's always thinking up things to do with us. Which made me surprised about something she said the other day when we were walking Eric home from the park. Well, Bex and I were walking – Eric was zipping off in all directions.

'He's like a boomerang, this brother of yours,' Bex said, grabbing his jacket the next time he passed and holding onto him so we could cross safely at the lights. And then she said the surprising thing, which was, 'You know, Princess, I reckon we should be doing more stuff with Eric.' Bex often calls me Princess, which is a bit of a tease because of Eric's dragon games, but it's a nice one. If I did mind I'd ask her not to – I wouldn't be shy of doing that. But I also like it when she calls me Eliza, which is my real name, because almost no one uses that, not even Dad. I'm mostly Lizzie to everyone.

But I was majorly amazed by her saying we should do more with Eric, because we already do tons with him every day. Bex picks him up from school and the two of them mostly go straight off on their own to the park, or the canal, or sometimes to the wildlife reserve over the railway bridge. Sometimes they meet me after my school finishes, or I join them if I'm not going off with Susie, who's my best friend from school. The thing is, Eric's happiest when Bex and I are both around. He tends to worry when someone important in his life goes missing, which was a big problem when he started school, although he's a lot better now. Anyway, like I say, it's easier to please him than not.

I can tell most adults think Eric's spoiled. I think he is too, but not very. It's hard not to let him do what he wants because he's so sweet most of the time and you want to please him, and keep him happy. Bex indulges him too; it isn't just me. Dad doesn't *seem* to spoil him much, but on the other hand he gives in to him a lot of the time. We're all on Eric's team, is what Bex says. Sometimes when he's being especially demanding she bows low to him and says, 'Anything you say, Your Highness, your wish is my command,' and I think she's being rather sarcastic, but Eric thinks she's only joking, and he just giggles at her and bows low back, and then everyone laughs.

When Bex and I take him out we're laden down like pack ponies with all his gear: his folding scooter and his backpack and his jacket and his sports gear, and all his safety stuff like kneepads and a helmet. Bex says it's more like being the pit-stop team for a racing driver than a pack pony, because Eric zooms around and then rushes back to find us and swap his ball for the scooter, or grab a drink of water. Then off he goes again at top speed. I don't know how Bex manages when she's got him alone; I often have trouble with him by myself. But when I ask she just grins and says, 'Piece of cake, Princess.' I think she's got him sussed better than I have. When it's your little brother it's harder to cope.

Sometimes, to even things up, Susie comes along and we take our skates to Regent's Park and go off along the pavements. You can get a good rhythm going, and really whizz along. Eric doesn't have skates yet, thankfully – if he did he'd probably mow everyone down or fall into the flowerbeds. What he wants next is actually a bike, and I think Dad will probably get him one for his birthday, but he'll need stabilisers to start with and I bet he won't want to use them. I'm getting ready for the arguments.

Anyway, when Bex said that surprising thing about how we should be doing more with him, it turned out that what she meant wasn't anything to do with going to the park or playing games, it was about taking him to museums and art galleries. 'Like your mum would have done,' Bex added. And she's right about that, although she never knew Mum – she only knows what Dad's told her. But I know that Mum would have done those things with Eric because she did them with me. I remember her taking me to art shows and museums, and once to hear a proper poet read his poems in our local library up in Cambridge. Eric came to the poetry too, actually, but he was tiny then and he doesn't remember. I know he doesn't because I read one of the poet's poems to him the other day, and then I asked him if he'd heard it before, and he said he hadn't.

Bex said, 'Eric gets oodles of physical exercise, but he doesn't get enough of a brain workout. He needs more of a challenge in that department.' I don't think she should be worried because there's nothing wrong with Eric's brain. But she explained what she meant, which was that Eric's brain needed stretching and building up, just like his legs and arms. 'He lives inside his head most of the time, making up stories,' she added. 'He needs something to get his mental teeth into.'

'Grr!' said Eric loudly, who was suddenly right behind us. 'Look out, you two, I'm a fire-breathing, princess-eating dragon again! Going – to – eat – you – UP!'

'See what I mean?' said Bex, untangling his scooter from her shoulder bag. 'See?' And I have to say, I do see.

Dad worries about Eric too. I know, because when Dad's building up to major worrying his eyebrows squash together and he runs his hand through his hair about fifty times a minute. He does that a lot when Eric's being tricky. I understand why, all right – it's because of Mum dying and Dad having to be a single parent 24/7, which I can see must be tiring and encourage his anxious thoughts. I think it's a waste of his energy to worry as much as he does, although I don't expect him to stop, that's just he way he is. I'm a worrier myself so I understand the problem. But I also think, why worry about Eric *so* much? He's not going to stay this way for ever. He'll grow up soon and get more sensible. Except I know the answer, really. Dad's just Dad, and Eric's Eric, and Eric pushes all Dad's worry-buttons at once.

Because of Dad's particular kind of full-on worrying, just to give you one example, we don't have a car of our own any more. We did have one but Dad sold it before we moved down to London. When we go anywhere we walk or use buses and the underground, or sometimes if we're in a terrific hurry we go in a taxi, which Eric loves and I enjoy for the novelty value. Dad tells people we do without a car to help the environment, but I know that's not the only reason. We aren't even really supposed to get lifts with friends, not unless Dad says we can. He doesn't trust them. Not the friends – the cars.

2

I don't remember a lot from when Mum was alive. I know where we lived – it was up near Cambridge – and I know what the house looked like. I remember how the handrail on the staircase had a wooden ball at the corner where it turned; I used to give it a pat every time I passed. But if I say 'Cambridge' to myself, it's like looking back down a tunnel to another world. If I concentrate I can remember how living in that world felt, like having a taste of something in your mouth that you used to love eating and don't eat any more.

I do remember how it was right after Mum died, but that's not a good memory so I try not to have it. If I skip over that I can get straight to when Dad told me we were moving to London, and after that Dad started being Dad again, and we all stopped being miserable every second of every day and stopped crying so much. Well, Dad and I cried less, anyway. Eric didn't because he was teething as well as missing Mum, and he was too little to understand what was going on.

That morning Dad said he'd sold our house and found a flat near a park in London, and it'd just be the three of us together. 'Just us three,' he told me, his voice croaky from so much miserableness. 'Us against the world, Lizzy darling. I'll look after you, and you'll look after me, and we'll both look after Eric.' He hugged me when he said that, and I hugged him back as hard as I could because I wanted him to know it would be OK, and a big hug can make you feel that's true.

Dad didn't have a job when we first got to London, but then he got one and put Eric into a day nursery, because there wasn't anyone to look after him. Eric didn't mind: he was too young to know what else could happen and anyway, he liked being with other babies. Dad took me to school every day, and then he dropped Eric off at the nursery. In the afternoons we had a child minder who picked me up from school and collected Eric from nursery, and then Dad took over again when he got home from work. It was a plan, like Dad said at the time, and mostly it worked.

But the child minder couldn't always wait for

Dad if he ran late at work, or if he needed to go to the supermarket on the way home. And it got harder when Eric started school, because then he was older and knew what was what, and he hated not having me or Dad take him there or pick him up afterwards. My school was in a different street so I couldn't even see him at lunchtime. Suddenly our lives didn't fit other people's routines and they didn't fit what any of us really wanted, either. I expect that happens to other families in our situation.

So Dad looked around for an au pair who'd be there for us more often. We went through a bunch of them, one after the other, for the next couple of years. At first we weren't lucky, and none of them worked out for long. Eric didn't like the first two and, like Dad said, when Eric's not happy, *no one's* happy. The next one was better but she had to go back to Spain, and the one after that smacked me just for not eating broccoli, which I didn't want because she'd cooked it for so long it had gone yellow and smelly. When Dad found out about the smack he sent her away and made me promise to say if anyone else was mean to me. Then it was his turn not to like the next one, although I've forgotten why.

But last year our luck changed for the better. We

got Bex! Eric liked her straight away, which was a considerable relief all round. I like Bex too, *and* I like having her look after us, and it's soothing to know for sure what the arrangements are going to be before they happen. She kind of belongs to us because we're her job. So we rely on her, and she relies on us. I know it won't be for ever, because Bex is training to do reflexology, which is a therapy treatment. She's learning to massage people's feet in a certain way, which she says can raise your energy levels, and even cure other bits of you like a sore shoulder or a headache. And when Bex has passed her final exams she'll probably want to leave us and do reflexology all the time. I do know that. But in the meantime, which is right now, it's great.

Bex doesn't live with us. There isn't room; we need all our bedrooms just for the three of us. But she shares a flat down in Camden. Well, actually, we're in Camden too, but in a different part of it. Our block of flats is next to the edge of Regent's Park where the zoo is, and Bex lives further north – along our road and down Parkway and then up almost as far as Kentish Town. So she catches a bus to us, or sometimes she walks, every weekday morning. And when she arrives, Dad can leave for work.

First of all Bex checks that Eric has clean clothes

on, and that he's got everything he needs for school that day. And she makes him finish his breakfast if he hasn't already, and then she walks him to the school gate, or right into his classroom if he wants her to, which he often does. No one has to make me finish my breakfast – I like eating too much – and no one needs to check my clothes are clean or walk me to school. Eric is the main part of Bex's job, no question.

After she's delivered Eric to school Bex goes back to our flat and does some of our housework and shopping. She takes over things we can't do ourselves, even though the three of us all do jobs like making our beds, and putting our dirty clothes straight into the laundry basket and not on the floor. Later, while we're still at school, Bex goes to her reflexology classes, and after that it's time to pick Eric up and entertain him, which is how she describes it, or 'keep him from annoying the rest of the world for a while', which is what Dad says.

Bex usually cooks our dinner too, ready for when Dad gets home, and I help with that if I haven't got too much homework. I have learned how to make her pasta sauce and her salad, and she's teaching me to make veggie soup as well. You can almost stand a spoon up in her soup – it's as good as a stew. Sometimes Bex stays and has dinner with us. She used to do that a lot when she first started. She even used to stay after Eric and I were in bed so she and Dad could talk. But now everything's working smoothly and Bex mostly leaves as soon as Dad's home. I think that probably means Dad's more relaxed and she doesn't need to check in with him so much.

It's a bit of a jigsaw puzzle slotting our lives together, but it mostly works out in the end. If there's a glitch, Mrs Oliver from downstairs sits with us until Dad gets in, or we go to her flat and watch TV or play with her cat. I like being there because Mrs Oliver doesn't hassle you or hover around watching in case you break something. She sets us up in her living room and then says, 'Sing out if you need anything, my dears,' and goes off to phone her daughter, or sometimes she makes us a cake. One time, when Bex had flu, one of her friends came instead of her for two whole weeks and that worked fine too, because Mack was an ace hamburger cook *and* he made Eric manage his scooter properly in the park; Eric won't listen to me or Bex about that.

School holidays are still a bit of a puzzle for us to solve. Dad takes time off from work but he doesn't get as much holiday as we do and we have to fill in the gaps with extra Bex, and clubs in the park and the leisure centre. In emergencies we get child minders all over again, and I hope that doesn't happen with the holiday that's coming up soon. I'm old enough now to be left in charge, which I have pointed out, but I don't think Dad will agree easily because of worrying about what might happen, and also because he doesn't want to put everything on me; he says it isn't fair. It doesn't worry me about being fair or not. I just don't want to be child-minded all over again, when I'm not one.

'You're not a grown-up either, Lizzie,' Dad said, when I tried to explain how I felt. 'Don't carry the whole world on your shoulders just because you can. Be young! Laugh and be merry, why don't you?' And he grinned and tickled me to make his point. I am so majorly ticklish that I crumple up and can't stop giggling and I have to give in right away. It's a burden.

But mostly being just the three of us works OK: we manage fine almost all the time. And although Dad worries about Eric not having a mum, and about me doing too much looking after Eric and not enough looking after myself, and...well, you name it and Dad's eyebrows will start squashing together about it. Bex says, 'Don't *you* worry too, Princess Lizzie. There's quite enough worrying done in this household already. Your dad's a good guy and he's doing his best, which is more than a lot of people do in this life.' Bex likes to look on the bright side and is keen on people doing their best. She says that to Eric when he's being a pain about doing something perfectly, and not seeing that you usually have to practise a bit first.

'Nervy, your Eric, isn't he?' is what our neighbour Mrs Oliver says when he's all edgy and up in the air. I know she thinks he's young for his age because I heard her saying he was babyish to her daughter on the phone when she didn't mean me to hear. To be fair to Mrs Oliver, she does like Eric, especially when he's being charming, which he often is. 'He could charm the socks off a snake,' she once said, which shows how much she really admires him underneath.

The trouble is, Eric's always been my pet. I've always treated him like a baby, so if he acts like one it's partly my fault. I was so excited when Mum was pregnant, I could hardly wait for Eric to be born and I helped a lot when he was a baby. I held the bottle for him when he was having a feed and I'd pass cotton wool and baby wipes to Mum when she was cleaning him up. I helped him learn to walk, and I heard the very first word he ever said. I know girls at school who bully their little brothers and change the rules of a game halfway through to stop them winning, but I've never wanted to do that to Eric.

Susie teases me about it. She says Eric's got me in his pocket and I'll have to climb out one day, but I'm not sure she's right.

Anyway, like I was saying, being Just Us Three works out: 'all for one and one for all', like Dad says. Just Us doesn't include child minders of course, and it doesn't actually include Bex either, although she's more one of us than anyone else is. If I'm honest, she really is the number four in our household, but the trouble with that is that Mum was number four, and I don't think anyone else can take over her number. Maybe Bex could be number five, except that would make us notice the hole where number four was even more than we already do, so it's best if we stay Just Us Three. Sometimes I wonder if Dad and Bex could get together as an item, and then Bex could come and live with us all the time and she could still be a reflexologist but she'd be part of our family as well. I'd like that. At least I think I would. I only wonder if I really *truly* would like it, because I enjoy having Dad to myself. Apart from sharing with Eric of course, but that's different, I do that anyway.

Susie's mum got married again and Susie likes Neil, that's her new father. She says he's really quite OK, and she even likes her stepsister Mia, who's in Eric's year, although not in his class. But Susie also told me in confidence that she liked it better when it was just her and her mum together, after her first dad left. She hasn't told her mum that because she feels rather mean about thinking it, and she knows it would upset her. I shouldn't really repeat a confidence, but you don't know Susie, so it's probably safe enough.

Dad's had girlfriends since we came to London, but I don't think they've been serious. He didn't have one for ages, and then he started going out with a woman from work, Sara. She was OK. She came out with us at the weekends for a while, and Dad got baby-sitters a couple of nights a week so they could go out to a movie together or to the theatre, things like that. Like I say, she was OK, but I didn't like it all *that* much that Dad was seeing her, and anyway it didn't last. There was another one last year, a dancer called Elsa, but she joined a dance company and went back to Sweden, and we don't see her any more. They still email each other though, because they're still friends. Elsa's very pretty, and she taught me a good salad – different from Bex's but also very tasty; Elsa's had dried cranberries in it. She also taught me how to do handstands. But I'd still rather have Dad to myself.

3

Tonight I overheard Eric telling his memory box what he'd done at school today. He was mixing what he wished had happened – like taking a rocket trip into space – with news about how smelly his classroom is, and learning to count in fives which he's just getting the hang of. So it was dragons and spiders and *vroom vroom* noises from a new motorised space-dragon he's invented, and a bit about counting to one hundred in fives being easy-peasy, and starting to do that backwards and getting stuck. And then pretending he wasn't stuck at all and switching back to dragon noises.

I don't worry about Eric talking to the memory box like that, although I don't like it at all when he talks out loud to Mum instead. I know I shouldn't mind, but I do. After Mum died, and before we moved to London, Dad took me to a doctor to talk about missing Mum. She was OK, the talk doctor; she didn't *make* me talk about it and I didn't want to, so mostly I drew pictures. But one thing I remember was her saying I should go ahead and talk to Mum in my head, if I wanted to. 'She'd like that,' I remember her telling me. 'Your mum would like to know you hadn't stopped thinking about her and wanting to talk to her.' So I expect Mum's pleased that Eric does it, and if he just did it inside his head, like I still do, I wouldn't have to know and then I wouldn't mind. I'm not saying it makes him weird or anything, but I do find it creepy when he chats away to Mum like she's actually in the room. He doesn't do it in front of other people, though, which would be worse.

But after he heard about the Mythical Creatures exhibition he started to do it a lot – so you could say that everything I'm going to tell you, the whole story, started when Dad read about an exhibition that was coming to the Natural History Museum in London. I'd never have known a whole chain of things could start from something like that. Like when you drop a stone into a pond, and the ripples spread out but you don't see where they go. Or like when someone in a book accidentally says a magic word, a word they didn't know was magic, and they're transported to another world.

Who knew it could happen in real life?

So. It all began on an ordinary Saturday morning when we were having what Dad calls a 'slow breakfast'. That means the three of us were sitting around in our living room eating toast and honey, and listening to the radio or reading the newspaper (Dad), drawing dragon pictures (Eric), and doing more Aussie knitting (me: I was making one long multicoloured tube, to sew into a spiral and make Susie a hat for her birthday).

On weekdays we have cereal and fruit for breakfast, and freshly-squeezed juice if there's time. Dad has developed what he calls his 'working method' for weekday breakfasts. Before he did we used to stumble round getting in each other's way and ending up late for school and work, or not eating breakfast at all which isn't good for you. But now it's fine because Dad has a system. He gets up early and preps everything. Then he wakes us up and we come out and finish it off. Like, depending on the fruit of the day Eric peels oranges and bananas, or I cut apples and pears into slices. And if we run late then Bex helps when she arrives. But at the weekends we take longer over breakfast and sit around together. And that's when we tell Dad about school things if there's anything to tell, or we say what we'd like to do with him over the weekend, and if he can make it happen then he does.

Anyway, that Saturday morning Dad suddenly said, 'Hey, this'll interest you, Eric. Listen.' And he read out an article from the paper about an exhibition that was coming from New York to the Natural History Museum in London. We've been to that museum together when Eric was mad about dinosaurs, which were his first big passion. And I went with my class when we were doing mini-beast projects because, believe it or not, there's a whole permanent exhibition about mini-beasts, too. Imagine that! Dinosaurs and mini-beasts in the same building! It just goes to show that natural history is teeny-tiny as well as majorly enormous.

'The new show's called "Mythical Creatures",' Dad explained. 'It's about creatures from old-time legends, things like dragons, unicorns and mermaids,' he went on, watching Eric's eyes get wider and wider, and then reaching out to ruffle his hair. 'Your sort of thing, eh, curly top?'

'When, Dad?' asked Eric, ignoring the hair-ruffle which would usually annoy him. His voice was husky with excitement and he'd dropped his coloured pencils. 'Can we go today?'

Dad explained that the exhibition didn't start until just before the school holidays. 'But I'll take you all right, don't you worry,' he promised. 'We can all go if you like – you'd like it too, Lizzy, I should think. Maybe even Bex, as well.'

The idea of Mythical Creatures got Eric stirred up. We had to look up unicorns and mermaids in the encyclopaedia and find pictures of them on the internet. Eric was fascinated with unicorns, which were new to him; he liked that they were like ponies, only a lot more exotic. Mermaids were another new thing. The next time we played his dragon game I had to be a mermaid tied to a rock, instead of a princess.

'At least you don't have to be a unicorn,' Bex said with a grin, helping to untie me. 'That horn can really weigh you down.'

Then Eric came home with a note from school, to say that the whole of his year were going to see Mythical Creatures when it opened. You'd think he'd have been over the moon about that, but he wasn't. He'd worked himself up into a state because he thought he'd have to choose who to go with. He didn't know which he wanted more: to go with everyone in his class, or go with us in the holidays, and he was just about beside himself with frustration. 'What'll I do?' he wailed. *I don't know what to do!'*

Bex is good with Eric when he's in a tizzy. She gets in close and makes him look at her, and she keeps her voice low and calm, and mostly he copies her and relaxes again. She did all that, but he still wouldn't eat his after-school snack, and he sobbed when he stubbed his toe in the park, which he wouldn't usually care about. But when Dad heard about the problem he just said that Eric could go to the exhibition twice, or even a hundred times, if he wanted to, and then Eric was happy again. Sometimes Dad can please him when no one else can.

That night, Eric told the memory box about Mythical Creatures. He'd left his door open for Dad to come and read him a story and put his light out. I wasn't eavesdropping; I could hear him from my room without even trying. 'I'll bet they've got enormous dragons, as big as bendy buses,' he said. 'And I'll learn lots more about them, and I'll get better and better at doing them, and I'll breathe real fire and everything.' Then he lowered his voice a bit, like he was talking confidentially to someone, although I could still hear him. Whispering isn't one of Eric's talents. 'And you'll be proud of me,' he went on. 'Because I'm going to find your Saint George and stick him back where he belongs.'

That last bit gave me a bit of a fright. You might think it's no weirder to talk out loud to a person who isn't there than it is to talk to a box. And OK, they're probably about equal in the weirdness stakes, but when I catch Eric talking to Mum it makes me feel funny. That's all I'm saying.

I knew what he was talking about, the Saint George thing. He used to play with the dragon chain ages ago, but when he got keen on dinosaurs it had gone back into the memory box. I'd noticed it had come out again now that he'd heard about a dragon exhibition. The dragon chain is actually a medallion on a chain that Dad found in Mum's jewellery box, and to be truthful it's only half a medallion. It's carved in metal so the detail stands out, and the figure on the half that Eric has, is a dragon. Dad said that originally it showed both Saint George *and* the dragon, but the Saint George half had broken off so only the dragon was left. But for some reason, Mum had kept the broken bit.

Dad told me about Saint George, too. He was a Christian saint who lived hundreds and hundreds of years ago, and Dad said that maybe he wasn't a real person or an actual saint at all: just a hero in a story. But anyway, the story goes that Saint George killed a dragon that was threatening to destroy a whole village. The village leaders had tied a princess – they just happened to have a spare one handy, Dad said – to a rock on the seashore. They thought the dragon would eat the princess and go away again, without coming right into the village and eating everyone else.

As if! is what I think about that. I'd have thought the dragon would be more likely to develop a taste for humans when it gobbled up the princess, and it would have looked around for more of them. But the story says that at the very moment the dragon arrived breathing fire and licking its lips at the sight of the princess, Saint George galloped up on his horse, killed the dragon, and saved her. So that's how Saint George is always shown in pictures: on a horse, waving his sword at a dragon. Sometimes the princess is there too, standing around looking grateful.

'You can see where Saint George is missing at the side, here, see? He got broken off years ago,' Dad said when he first showed it to me. 'But it was important to your mum, and Eric might like to have it when he's older. The dragon's well done.' Dad's right; the carving on the dragon is good. It's lashing its tail and looks really fierce.

And now Eric wanted to wear it all the time again. I just hoped it didn't get more broken than it already was; he's not the most careful person in the world. But then again it was his, after all, and he could wear it if he wanted to – just not to school because you're not allowed jewellery and the dragon chain counts. All that week he forgot it was forbidden at school, or more likely he didn't want to take it off and so he didn't. He wore it under his uniform so you couldn't see it. Then Bex got wise to him, and started checking for it before they left the flat.

The first time Eric got the medallion out of his box we looked at it together, and he said a very Eric-y thing. I explained about the Saint George bit that was missing. He ran his finger over the wobbly edge where Saint George would have been, and said, 'I'll find it for her.'

I didn't understand at first – because Eric said 'her', I wondered if he thought Saint George was a woman. But it turned out he meant that he was going to find the missing half of the medallion for Mum. I started to explain that she hadn't had that bit of it either; that the Saint George half had broken off when Mum was little, but then I stopped myself. I think it's hard for Eric when everyone else – well, Dad and me anyway, which is everyone else in this case – knows all about Mum. Everything that's available to know. And Eric doesn't know anything in the same way, because he doesn't remember her.

I'd hate that, if it was me being reminded all the time about how I was the one who didn't know.

After all, if he wanted to make up a story for himself about finding the missing half of the medallion, why not? Who would it hurt? And to be honest I'm not exactly sure I could have stopped him doing it if I tried, even if I'd told him that the missing half had been lost for years and years. Like Dad says, Eric doesn't let facts get in the way of one of his stories.

4

The next night I heard a fox barking on our railway line, so Dad and I hung out my bedroom window trying to see where it was. We've watched the railway foxes before, and they're great. You'd think they might rather live in the wildlife reserve, but they seem to prefer life beside the railway track. Fewer people around, is what Dad says. He thought they'd have cubs again, and I wanted Eric to see them. Dad wanted that too – as a good distraction from mythical creatures. He hoped he could get Eric interested in wildlife. 'Give him something real to think about,' is what Dad said.

You might wonder why I just said 'our' railway line: it sounds as though we own one, which isn't true, of course. But the main line out of Euston Station, which goes north to Scotland, runs behind our block of flats. Dad bought our flat before he knew if the noise of the trains would bother us, and after the deal went through he started to worry about it, like you sometimes do when it's too late. He finally realised that our flat was cheaper than others near Regent's Park because the railway put people off. He got so worried he said that if the noise turned out to be a problem, well, we'd just move again! Another *as if*, I reckon, like the dragon eating the princess and not wanting more people to eat. How likely is it that anyone would go through all that moving hassle all over again when they've only just done it? I didn't think that at the time because I was only seven, and if we'd really had to move again I'd just have thought: OK, *as long as I don't lose my teddy*.

But Dad needn't have worried, because the train noise doesn't bother any of us. After a couple of weeks I didn't even notice that trains were rushing past my window, and noticing turns out to be a lot more important than actually hearing them. Eric doesn't remember living without trains outside the window, so he's not bothered, and anyway he turns the train noises into dragons in his imagination.

You could worry that the three of us will turn into train spotters and stand at the window with bobble hats and clipboards, noting down train numbers. That hasn't happened, but I do like looking out at the railway line from my bedroom. In the summer you can't see the tracks because trees block the view. But in the autumn and winter, when their leaves have fallen, you can see right across the line to the houses on the other side, and it's interesting. You can see the light of TV screens if people leave their blinds up, but you can't see much else unless it's summer and they're out in their back gardens having a barbecue or gardening. Eric especially loves to watch the barbecues; he's rather fussy about food but I think he'd eat a cardboard box if it came off a barbecue. And on firework night last year one of the houses opposite had a big party in their garden with rockets, and we put out the lights in our flat and stood at the window in the dark and enjoyed the show.

I don't want you to think I'm secretly watching people out my window like some kind of stalker. I wouldn't look through Dad's binoculars or anything like that. It's just . . . that's the view out my window and I'm more or less bound to take notice. At night, when I'm doing my homework and the trains go past, and the lights are on inside the carriages, I sometimes try to pick out just one person, and make up a story about them. Mostly you can't do it because the trains go too fast; you can only focus on individual people if the train stops and waits for the signals to change. Which, as it happens, they often do, right outside my bedroom window.

Anyway, back to the foxes. When we heard that fox bark, Dad and I would have gone straight out to look for it, if we could. We usually go along to the railway bridge because from there you can see right up the line and along both sides of the tracks. But of course we couldn't go out because we couldn't leave Eric by himself, even though he was fast asleep. So Dad promised we'd all go out before Eric's bedtime later in the week and he'd take his binoculars. Sometimes it's easier to see things in the evening light with binoculars, instead of just your eyes.

Dad's taught us to stay quiet and still when we're spotting wildlife, and to concentrate on looking for something which moves or stands out from its surroundings. Sometimes the something turns out to be an old plastic bag or a heap of leaves, but other times, if you're lucky, it's a fox. The cub I saw the year before was the best wild thing I'd ever seen. It was so sweet and fluffy – it looked like a toy. Seeing a fox cub makes you think you'd like one as a pet, even though I know I wouldn't actually like it if I did have one because of the fleas which they always have, or lice or mange which are even worse, and because it wouldn't be so cute in our small flat.

Anyway, foxes are wild animals, and I think they should stay wild if they can, even though living beside a London railway line and scavenging food from rubbish bins isn't as wild as country foxes are. I know some people hate having foxes in towns and go on about how dirty they are and how they dig up your garden and scare your pets. But honestly, they *look* so gorgeous, and they're so smart, you can't help admiring them.

Eric missed the two females and one cub that Dad and I saw last year. He hadn't actually seen any of them yet, although waiting to see them was the one thing he was patient about. Dad said it showed he can do it if he wants to, but I knew that anyway. Eric can do most things once he sets his mind to it, and he notices more than you might think. When I told him what we'd seen that time, he picked up on the fact that there was a baby fox and two vixens, but no dad.

'Well, there must *be* a dad,' I pointed out. 'We just haven't seen him yet. And maybe the females baby-sit each other's cubs, like the meerkats on TV.' And Eric grinned and said, 'Maybe the daddy fox has to go to conferences,' which is what our dad does a lot. Then he added, 'Do foxes even have, like, a mum and a dad together?' I was surprised he'd thought about that, and I wondered if he'd started to notice other families and see that they can be different from your own. It happens.

'Well, for all we know they might be *exactly* like an ordinary human family when they're at home,' I suggested. 'But maybe the dad fox has to be away at conferences, like you say. And when he is, then maybe Violet Vixen comes to stay with Viv Vixen and helps look after the baby, because...'

'Because Viv's doing a reflexology course!' Eric finished with a grin.

I remembered Mum once read me a poem about a fox, and I looked for it to read to Eric. It said something about a fox touching a leaf with its nose, and I had seen one of the vixens doing exactly that. But I couldn't remember more than that, not even who the author was, which made it almost impossible to find in a book. Bex was baby-sitting us because Dad was – yes! – at a conference dinner, and when I told her what I was looking for she tried to remember a fox poem she knew when she was little in Australia. She said her poem rhymed, and it was about foxes and sockses and cardboard boxes, but she couldn't remember more than that. I tried to track it down, but it was as hard as finding Mum's poem.

Bex told Eric two foxy jokes instead. 'What's the difference between fleas and foxes?' she asked, and

Eric shook his head. 'Foxes can have fleas,' said Bex, solemnly, 'but...' She paused and looked at him expectantly.

'But fleas can't have foxes!' he shouted, bouncing up and down in triumph. 'Tell me another one,' he begged, so Bex sat on his bed and thought for a minute.

'OK, what about this one. What is a fox's favourite dance?' she asked.

Eric didn't know and neither did I. It turned out to be something called a foxtrot, which I've never heard of, although Bex said they did it on those TV ballroom-dancing programmes. She kicked off her trainers and got up on her toes and started dancing round the room, but I thought it looked rather silly. She said she'd ask Dad if he knew how, and they could demo it together, but I don't think she'll have much luck with that. Dad doesn't do dancing, as far as I know.

By then Eric was getting way too lively for someone who was supposed to be settling down. In fact he started to get out of bed to do his own foxtrot, so I decided to use my magic spell on him. It usually works like a charm, so that's why I call it a spell. Also, it sounds like one. Mum used to say it to me when I was in bed before she put the light out, and now I say it to Eric. It's better not to use it too often – only when I need it, and I suppose that means I'm treating it like a real spell: one where the magic might get used up unless you're careful. It's from a longer poem, but this is the bit that does the business:

> *Seven fish in the sway of the water.*
> *Six candles for a king's daughter.*
> *Five sighs for a drooping head.*
> *Four ghosts to gentle her bed.*
> *Three owls in the dusk falling.*
> *Two tales to be telling.*
> *One spell for sleeping.*

There's a whole routine that goes with it. I sit on the edge of Eric's bed and hold up seven fingers ready to start – but I don't ever start until he's lying down properly, with his head on the pillow and the duvet pulled straight. And then I begin to say each line slowly and quietly, waiting for Eric to join in, which he does. And I fold down a finger after I've said a line, and then I say the next one and fold down another finger. And so on. I make my voice go slower and softer each time, and Eric's supposed to close his eyes when we get to the line about the owls because that's what I did with Mum. I say the very last line by myself and then I repeat it, and the second time Eric joins in. And by then he's always calmed down, and he turns on his side, and I turn off his light, and he's away.

Eric had nightmares when he first started school and that's when I started the spell with him, because Mum told me it was a spell against nightmares. I told Eric the same thing. He thinks Mum made the whole thing up – the spell, that is – and I've never said it's from a poem in a book, and not one of Mum's.

When Eric was asleep, Bex and I had an hour for just the two of us before I had to go to bed, too. I love time alone with Bex and I don't often get it. I keep nagging her to do reflexology on my feet and she won't, but she does rub my feet sometimes, which is nice, although it can feel like it's going to tickle, which is a worry. I rub hers as well and then we take turns to soak our feet in a basin of water, and paint our toenails. Last night Bex had little sample pots of polish in her bag and she painted each of my toenails a different colour! I think they look majorly cool and I wish I could show them off. I will show Susie tomorrow, but I'll have to take my socks off in the cloakroom to do it.

I've thought of asking Bex if Susie could come round one night, and we could talk about clothes and things. But Eric most probably wouldn't like it; he wants to share Susie with me, and Susie and I don't always want him to join in, and if he felt excluded he'd never co-operate. He'd make a fuss and refuse to go to sleep. I'm still thinking about how I could make it happen, but in the meantime I like it being only Bex and me. Bex helps me with clothes when I ask her to – not that I have that many, but she says it's always good to have another woman's opinion. Dad never complains if we have to go shopping, even though you can tell he's bored rigid as soon as he sets foot in a clothes shop. Also, Eric usually has to come too, and let me tell you, no one would *choose* to go shopping with Eric in tow; it's too exhausting to bear for very long.

5

Dad was right about Eric getting swept up into Mythical Creatures excitement – in fact he threw himself into it with a passion that surprised even me, and I'm used to his single-mindedness. Every night he wanted to find out something else about another mythical creature from the past, or go over the things he'd already discovered. He sneaked the dragon chain back to school, and for several days not even Bex realised.

'It'll be confiscated if the teachers see it,' Bex said. 'Then you'll be in trouble, matey. They might even keep it for the rest of the week, you know; they wouldn't necessarily give it back to you at the end of the day.'

But Eric was unrepentant. 'They didn't see it though, did they?' he pointed out calmly. 'That's because the dragon chain's part of my spell and it protects me.' And he added, 'Actually, it probably goes invisible when a teacher looks at it.' But I noticed that he left it at home again for a while after that.

When there was only a week to go before the exhibition, Eric was practically spinning off the planet with excitement, and most nights he went through one drama or another. One evening he sobbed for half an hour because our internet connection was down and he couldn't get onto the museum website. Another night his silver colouring pencil was missing, so he threw all the others in the bin. 'I'm not going to the exhibition at all now!' he wailed. 'This sucks!' The next night my plate of apple crumble looked bigger than his, and his lip started to quiver. 'That's so not fair!' he said. 'It's supposed to be *exactly the same* as mine! You *promised*!' And even when I'd swapped our plates he sulked his way through every mouthful. It was exhausting.

I told Bex it was hard to find the bright side, but she just laughed and said we had to stay calm and not encourage the emotional stuff. Dad tried to cope, but it's hard for him to sympathise with Eric's performances because Dad's not that kind of person himself. He tried to do his bit, though. He came home from work early every day to help avoid more crises, and he even went along to the school one morning to have a word with Ms Jerwood, and explain that Eric was likely to stay wound up until the class actually went on the trip.

'How was she?' I asked Dad afterwards. I'd had Ms Jerwood as a teacher myself and I remembered how kind she'd been to me. Dad said she'd been kind to him, too. 'She said it's not just Eric; everyone in the class is wound up,' Dad explained, running his hand through his hair. He'd been doing that so much lately his hair was sticking straight up like a punk rocker's. 'She thinks there's a special attraction for his age group to things which don't really exist like dragons and dinosaurs. "Safe to be scared of", is what she told me.'

I don't think that's true for Eric, because I don't think he's frightened of dragons at all. He just wanted to be one – *that* was what was making him super-excited. The night before his class trip, there was another crisis. I found Eric in his room throwing all his T-shirts on the floor, and his bottom lip was quivering again. He doesn't usually do a diva about clothes, but it turned out that he wanted to wear his Spiderman T-shirt to the exhibition under his uniform, but it was so old it had holes in it, and Bex had said he had to choose another one.

Luckily, I had an idea. 'You know what?' I said,

sitting down on his bed. 'I think Spiderman's luck has finally run out – so how about your dinosaur T-shirt? The one Dad got you with the dinosaur alphabet on the front?' It's actually a great T-shirt and I wish they'd had it in the museum shop in my size too. The alphabet goes from A for Ankylosaurus through to Z for Zephyrosaurus, with little pictures of them all. Luckily, it still fitted him.

'I bet the dragons will be impressed with all those dinosaurs,' I said, helping him take it off again. The tantrum warning signs had vanished, and Eric gave me an enormous grin. 'I'm going to wear my dragon chain as well,' he confided. 'They'll never see it, Ms Jerwood or the others, but the dragons will know it's there. It'll show I'm really one of them.' No way was I going to argue with that.

I don't suppose Eric slept much that night. He gets so wound up at Christmas and the night before his birthday that you think he'll go off, *TWANG!* like a spring. But he was exhausted with excitement by bedtime, so perhaps he just passed out. But next morning he was pale and didn't want any breakfast. Dad thought he might be sick if he ate anything, but Bex thought he'd be sick if he *didn't* eat, so she got a couple of mouthfuls of cereal into him. And then she whispered to him that as a special treat he could eat a banana in the street on the way to school. And of course Dad heard Bex's stage whisper like he was meant to, and he pretended to be so horrified that Eric giggled with delight and calmed down.

He was keen to be early for the museum bus and Bex knew he'd get panicky if there was a last-minute rush. She was patient while he checked three times to make sure he had his packed lunch, and enough money for the gift shop, and his notebook with the question sheets, and his dinosaur pencil case. And the breakfast-in-the-street banana. And then, at last, they were off.

I gave a cheer when the door closed behind them, and Dad gave a big sigh. He ran his hand through his hair again, and poured himself another coffee. His eyebrows started to smooth out right away, but his hair was still a mess. 'Boy oh boy, what a performance and a half,' he sighed. 'We're in for a whole new level in dragon-obsession now, Lizzie love. Brace yourself!'

I told him what Bex had said about unicorns being harder than princesses, and Dad laughed. 'That young woman's a treasure,' he said. 'We're lucky to have her. Anyone who can make you happy *and* deal with Eric and unicorns as well as dragons… Worth her weight in gold.'

'Don't forget the mermaids,' I reminded him. 'They take a fair bit of managing, too.'

Dad gave a theatrical shudder. 'Wet and slimy! Yuck! The Lord preserve us from having to deal with mermaids in the bath,' he said.

'You wouldn't have to clean up after them, though,' I pointed out. Cleaning the bathroom is one of my weekend jobs. Every Saturday morning, I do the bath and the basin and the mirror, and change the towels.

Dad grinned at me. 'All part of my master plan, Lizzie love,' he said. 'I know my limitations. Kitchens, bedrooms, laundry and vacuuming: I'm happy with all of 'em. But bathrooms? No way. A bridge and a half too far for me.'

I knew Eric would arrive home completely jazzed up, and bursting to tell us a thousand and one new things about mythical creatures. I wondered if he'd move on to unicorns once he'd seen them, or if maybe he'd be tempted back to dinosaurs when he'd had another look at the one in the entrance hall, the one that got him going in the first place. But the funny thing was, I was completely wrong. It didn't turn out that way at all.

I had the first clue when I got home and jogged up the eight flights of stairs to our flat. We'd had a talk about fitness at school the week before, and climbing stairs was top of the list of things to increase your stamina, so I was giving it a go. I couldn't run up them all yet, I got too puffed, but I was working on it. I found Bex in the kitchen, chopping veggies.

'Where's Dragon Boy?' I asked. 'Have we got a new mythical creature in the house?'

Bex smiled at me. 'Well, Princess Eliza,' she said, 'it hasn't turned out quite like I thought it would. We've got a new something all right, but I'm not sure exactly what it is. Have a look and tell me what you think.'

Eric was sitting on his bedroom floor and everything from the memory box was heaped in front of him. I saw all that but I didn't take much notice, because I just wanted to hear about his day. 'So?' I asked. 'How was it?'

'It was OK,' said Eric, without looking up. I thought he'd be fizzing with excitement and dying to tell me what he'd seen, but he wasn't. He seemed to be thinking about something else entirely. I didn't get it.

'Good dragons?' I suggested encouragingly. 'Fire-y ones with poisonous scales, and breathing smoke?' There was a silence. Eric still didn't look at me. He concentrated on sorting through the things in front of him, putting all the photos in one heap. He was being super-careful with everything, which was also unusual.

'Big monstrous ones with lots of teeth?' I prompted again. Eric finally glanced up and smiled at me in a sort of distracted way.

'It was OK,' he repeated politely. He sounded as though he was minding his manners with an adult – or like he was giving a talk in class about something he didn't care about. Then he started to gabble his words a bit, like you do when you just want to get through saying something boring and get back to something more interesting.

'I liked the big dragon best but there were others too. A Chinese one, with a spiky back like a pterodactyl, I liked that one. And we had lunch in a room with pictures of dragons all over the walls and the ceiling.'

Eric's delivery sounded odd, but the content was more like it. I went over to his bed, expecting him to launch into more stories about what he'd seen, but by the time I'd sat down he'd turned back to the pile of photos. He was going through them very slowly, looking at each one intently. There were a lot of them in his memory box now: photos of him as a baby; of all four of us when he was born; photos of just Mum or just Dad; photos of Eric and me with Dad at the zoo – the works, really. The whole Banks one-for-all-ers: the Original Four as well as Just Us Three.

I watched him, and I had the strangest feeling that he'd blanked me out; that he didn't even remember I was in the room. It was as if the exhibition and all the build-up to it had gone on in one world, and now Eric had stepped into a different world where ordinary things didn't interest him any more. Even when I got up again to leave, he didn't seem to notice. He didn't ask me to stay, or suggest a game, like he almost always did after school, especially if he thought my attention was flagging. Now it was *his* attention that was directed somewhere else.

I went back into the kitchen. Bex looked at me and raised her eyebrows, and I shrugged. 'I don't have a clue!' I said. I felt truly bewildered. 'I've never seen him like this before.'

'And he's been like that since I picked him up from school,' Bex said. She sounded bewildered too. 'All the other kids in his class were still leaping around shouting about what they'd seen, and there was Eric in the corner, in a little world of his own, not saying a word.'

I couldn't get my head round it. It was like Eric was excluding me from something, which had *never* happened before.

'Do you think something might have upset him today?' Bex suggested. 'Like, maybe he got overexcited on the bus and did something silly, and got ticked off big time? Or maybe one of the other kids was mean to him? Or maybe he's not feeling well... I did check to see if he had a temperature...' Her voice trailed away. I could tell she wasn't convinced by her own suggestions, and neither was I. Eric wasn't sad or resentful, like he was when something hurt his pride or upset his sense of justice. It was more like he had discovered a new and wonderful secret. But I told myself that if he had he wouldn't hold it to his chest for long; he never could.

'We'll find out soon enough,' I said, more confidently than I felt. 'I bet he'll say something to me, and we'll just wait until he does.'

The next day at school I asked Susie if Mia had liked the exhibition.

'She utterly loved it!' said Susie. 'Couldn't stop talking about it, about how she and her new best friend had shrieked their heads off when they walked into the first room and there was the biggest dragon they'd ever imagined, right in front of them.' She looked at me. 'I bet Eric was over the moon, wasn't he?' she asked. She knew about Eric and dragons. 'Sort of,' I said cautiously, and changed the subject. I wasn't ready to talk to Susie about it.

That night I overheard Eric talking to the memory

box in a different way – like he was having a proper two-way conversation with someone. He'd say something, and then he'd pause like he was listening to the reply, and then he'd say something back. It was like listening to one end of a phone conversation, and OK, that was definitely weird, but I wasn't majorly worried. I told myself it was just another aspect of being Eric, and having that vivid imagination which runs away with him. I reminded myself that I didn't know everything about him, even though sometimes I think I do. No one knows everything about another person – they can always surprise you.

Even Dad wasn't bothered by the changes in Eric, which for a man who worries as much as Dad does was reassuring. At least, I thought it was reassuring at first. Dad's theory was that Eric had finally had enough of dragons.

'All that excitement for weeks about the exhibition, and all the extra research he did?' Dad said. 'It filled his glass up right to the top. And so now – do you see? He's played out on dragons. He's had enough of 'em. Doesn't want to do 'em any more.' Dad paused, and then he added, 'Don't hold your breath though, Lizzie. Because there'll be something new on his horizon before we know it, and this time, I'm going to try to help him choose!'

I knew that Dad hoped Eric's new passion would be something real, like foxes. Dad's more comfortable with things he can see and touch; Mum was the one with imagination. But I also thought there was something wrong with Dad's explanation, although I wasn't sure exactly what. Somehow, though, what Dad said didn't fit how Eric was behaving, and I didn't believe he'd given up on dragons, either. He was still wearing the dragon chain and still pinning a dragon tail to the back of his T-shirt. It was true that he hadn't asked me to be a tied-up princess since he'd been to the exhibition, but I put that down to him being a bit distracted.

So I thought there must be a better explanation: I just didn't know what it was. But when Eric finally told me what was going on – what had happened at the museum – I was completely shocked. I hadn't seen the truth coming. I don't think anyone could have done.

6

Eric's secret spilled out a week later, when we went down to the railway bridge to look for foxes. Dad hadn't taken us before because the mythical creatures had got in the way, but Eric needed a nature project for school and I suggested the foxes because I'm interested in them myself. I knew I'd end up helping him, so it might as well be something I liked. Eric was keen right away, and Dad was keen too, for obvious reasons. But in the end Dad ran late at work and Bex was cooking dinner, so just the two of us went. It was a Friday night, so Eric could stay up to wait for Dad and then we'd all have dinner together, Bex included. And in the meantime there was enough daylight to look for foxes.

Eric was still unusually quiet, but I could sense an undercurrent of excitement fizzing away. It was like he was concentrating so hard on something else, he wasn't really with us. Like sleepwalking – you're there, but you're not there: *Earth to Eric*, kind of thing. I hoped the foxes would get him thinking about something else, instead of whatever was on his mind.

When we got to the railway bridge we dragged a pile of pizza boxes out from under the recycling bins. There are always boxes there because the slots in the paper and cardboard bin aren't big enough for them, so people stack them underneath. We piled the boxes up at the corner of the bridge, where the ground slopes and the wall's a bit lower. You can see over the wall if you stand on tiptoe, or on one of the benches, but it's better for fox-watching if you prop yourself against the wall and rest your elbows on it, and the boxes help get you up high enough. It's quite tricky to stack them, but I've worked out how to do it.

I took Dad's binoculars with us. They're valuable so I always carry them with the strap around my neck to be careful, and I trained them down the railway cutting. And right away I was lucky: there were two adult foxes and two cubs all together on the bank! I pointed down the line so Eric knew where to look and then put the binoculars around his neck so he could see them properly. The vision adjustment was right and he found the foxes right away. He sort of stiffened with excitement when he saw them, and then did little hops up and down to let me know that he had. I stopped him from hopping, though, because I thought he might slip off the pizza boxes and drop the binoculars.

We watched the foxes for what felt like ages, but it probably wasn't more than about twenty minutes. That mightn't sound a long time to you, but it is when you're standing as still as you possibly can on a stack of boxes, swapping binoculars back and forth, and hardly saying anything because of trying not to let the foxes know we were there. I don't think they did know, or in any case they weren't bothered. They're urban foxes after all; they're used to humans. But it's what Dad's taught us: to be still and quiet and not disturb them – so that's how we do it.

The foxes sat around casually like they were relaxing in their back garden. The two adults scratched a bit and nosed around on the ground, and played with the cubs which were rolling around looking cute and pouncing on tails and paws and whatever else they could find. And then finally one of the adults did an enormous stretch, like a cat, and trotted off along the railway line going north, looking like it knew exactly where it was going.

Foxes trot as though they're weightless; they're so light on their feet. I bet that foxtrot dance of Bex's isn't as good as the real thing.

'The fox went out on a chilly night,' Eric hummed under his breath, the next time we swapped the binoculars. I hadn't found the fox poems I'd been looking for but I'd remembered an old song about a fox going hunting for food for its babies, and taught it to Eric. He'd learned the whole thing really fast. You might even know it – it starts like this:

The fox went out on a chilly night,
And prayed for the moon to give him light,
For he'd many a mile to go that night,
Before he reached the town-o, town-o, town-o,
He'd many a mile to go that night,
Before he reached the town-o.

He ran 'til he reached a great big pen,
Where the ducks and the geese were put therein.
'A couple of you will grease my chin,
Before I leave this town-o, town-o, town-o,
A couple of you will grease my chin,
Before I leave this town-o.'

'It's not chilly, though,' I whispered back. 'And he

hasn't got many a mile to go to reach the town-o, either. He's already in it.'

'Not that far to the shops, either,' agreed Eric solemnly, and he was right. There's a row of shops up behind the next station, and I expect it's a good place for scraps and leftovers. Fox shopping.

And then I corrected what I'd said, because the adult foxes we were looking at were actually she's, not he's – the same ones I'd seen with Dad. '*She's* already in the town,' I added, still whispering. 'Dad says these are female foxes. They're called vixens.'

Even without using the binoculars I was certain they were the ones Dad and I had seen. One of them has a white chin and the other has a droopy ear, so they're easy to recognise. When White Chin left, Droopy Ear and the two cubs stayed where they were. The cubs curled up in a heap together and went to sleep, but Droopy Ear – the baby-sitter – sat and watched her leave, swivelling her ears back and forth and staring in that direction, even after White Chin was out of sight. I thought Droopy Ear looked sad about staying home to look after the babies. Dad would have said, *But that's a human idea, you can't apply it to wild animals.* But then, Dad wasn't there.

We decided we'd seen enough for one night, and we'd come back later in the week and try again. So we put the pizza boxes back, and Eric gave me the binoculars, and when I glanced down to see if he'd done up his jacket his eyes were shining with excitement. At first I thought it was because of the foxes, but then he grabbed my arm, and said in a low voice, 'I have something to tell you.' And then I realised he wasn't talking about foxes at all. He was going to tell me about whatever was on his mind! I felt pleased he was going to tell me before Dad or Bex. And I felt sort of protective towards him, like I mostly did, but also very curious about what he'd say. I bent down to him.

'What, Eric? What is it?' I prompted. I didn't want to put him off by being too pushy, but I didn't want him to change his mind, either.

'You know when I went to the museum?' Eric asked. I nodded encouragingly.

'I saw Mum,' he said.

I heard what he said, but it made no sense. I didn't understand what he meant at all. I stood and frowned at him, waiting for him to explain.

'Mum was there – in the museum,' he went on. 'She was in the gift shop, serving behind the counter.' He paused, but I just kept on staring at him, waiting for the meaning to click into place.

'You know, the counter near the writing paper that's made out of elephant poo,' he added helpfully. As if knowing which counter was involved would help.

'Eric…' I started to speak, although I didn't know what I was going to say. It didn't matter though: he was off in full flow.

'I didn't say anything to her right away,' he went on. Now he was talking fast with the words tumbling over each other. He'd kept this whole story to himself for days, and once he'd started talking he wouldn't stop until he'd got it all out.

'I was going to say hello to her,' he explained. 'But I wasn't sure at first that it was really her. Her being there – well, it took me by surprise.' He paused for a moment and looked down, fiddling with the zip on his jacket. My mind was frozen with astonishment. I know Eric and I know about his imagination, and if he'd said that he'd run into Spiderman at the museum, or that the diplodocus skeleton in the entrance hall had spoken to him, I'd have known what to say back. But this was different. I wanted to think he was joking, but I could tell he wasn't.

'So I stood and watched her for a while,' Eric went on. 'And after that, I *was* sure.' He paused again, and then he said, very calmly, 'It really was exactly her, Lizzy. It was Mum. I know it.'

'And then what happened?' I asked. My voice

sounded quite normal, just like I was asking an ordinary question, even though it wasn't ordinary, and I wasn't even sure I wanted an answer.

'Well, then they said we had to go and eat our lunch in the room with dinosaurs on the walls,' Eric explained. 'So we did, and I swapped one sandwich with Sim but otherwise I ate everything I had.' He sounded slightly defensive about that. Eric could be picky about food, and Bex didn't like it when he didn't finish his packed lunches or when he swapped items with friends: she thought he'd eat junk food and get hyperactive. She always got him to approve everything that went into his lunchbox.

'And afterwards,' he went on, 'Ms Jerwood said we could go back to the shop one last time if we were quick about it. So I did that.' Eric looked up again, and his expression was suddenly almost tragic. 'I was going to show her my dragon chain,' he said, 'so she'd know it was me.' He gave an enormous sigh. 'But she wasn't there any more. She'd gone.'

He held up a finger to show he hadn't finished his story. *Just like Ms Jerwood*, I thought distractedly, and not that he needed to keep my attention like that, I was listening so hard I'd almost stopped breathing.

'But I thought she was probably just having her lunch,' he added. 'And we had to get on the bus again, so I didn't get another chance.' He'd obviously worked it all out.

'Did – um, did she see you, too? When she *was* there, the first time?' I asked.

Eric shook his head. 'I don't think so. But she wouldn't recognise me now, would she, Lizzie? She hasn't *seen* me since I was a tiny baby. That's why I thought if I showed her the dragon chain...' His voice trailed off, and he glanced down.

I squatted in front of him and put my hands on his shoulders. 'Eric,' I said, and shook him gently. 'Come on. Look at me.'

He shoved his hands in his pockets, took a big breath, and looked back at me. He wasn't on the edge of laughing like he often was when he was making up one of his elaborate stories. Right now he was calm and solemn, but somehow excited with it. *He really believes this*, I thought. *He actually believes what he's saying.*

'Eric...' I started off, but then I stopped again. It was difficult to know what to say, but –

'It wasn't Mum,' I finally said, very firmly. 'You didn't see Mum.' But Eric just tilted his head and stared back at me.

'How do you know that?' he asked, reasonably. 'You weren't there. And you didn't see her.'

'Because – well, because it couldn't have been.'

I shook him gently again; I didn't want to upset him but I did want his attention. 'Be sensible! You *know* why not, Eric.'

But he didn't seem to take that in. Eric often acts more like a five-year-old than his real age, but he suddenly looked older than he actually is. Maybe it was because he was so matter-of-fact about what he was saying; so steady and sure about it.

'Why not?' he asked calmly. 'Why can't I be right? I know what she looks like too, you know. She's my mum as well as yours.'

7

Afterwards I wondered what would have happened
– and if things would've turned out differently in the
end – if I'd gone ahead right then, and insisted on
what I knew was the truth. If I'd just kept on at Eric
until I *made* him admit that he'd imagined it. *Eric, it
wasn't Mum*, I could have said again, more
definitely. *You didn't see her. You know that really;
you know she's dead. This is just your imagination
running away with you, like it does. Forget it.*

But I didn't say that to him, that night. I thought
I would at first, but I hesitated and then I finally
bottled out. And you have to ask: why not? Why not
right then and there? And my honest answer has
different parts to it. Because I didn't want to
disappoint him or take the shining excitement out
of his eyes. Because at first I didn't think it would do
any harm if he pretended that he'd seen Mum. And

because I still thought it was sad he couldn't remember her for himself. It's not his fault, and he shouldn't always have to be the one who's wrong. Because, of course, I knew he *was* wrong, and I realised what must have happened. He'd seen someone who looked like the photos of Mum we have all over the flat – and in his memory box, for that matter. Photo Mum's the only one he knows. And by the time he could have realised that he'd made a mistake, well, by then he'd decided to go for it anyway – hook, line and sinker. He was so worked up about the mythical creatures and all that excitement, and his imagination had got stuck in top gear. And *that's* why he thought the woman he'd seen in the museum shop was Mum.

If I'm completely honest, though, I have to say there was another big reason why I didn't insist right away that he was wrong, and didn't make him admit it. It has to do with how I'd felt after he'd said it. Even though I *knew* he must be wrong, it was a horrible shock to have him say it, like being tossed into an icy-cold bath. And *of course* he was wrong, there couldn't be any doubt about it. But right from that first moment there was always a little voice in my head, saying: *But what if he's right?* So I was trying to deal with my own feelings as well as Eric's, and not being sure how to do either of those things.

And that's the real reason I didn't go on at him.

Not even on the way home, when he said, 'Now that I've found her, Lizzie, she can come home again, can't she? Once we've told her where we live?' And I hadn't known what to say, but I knew I should talk to Dad about it, which I did the same night, after Eric was in bed and Bex had gone home. When it came to the moment, though, I almost didn't tell him after all. Maybe it would be better to talk to Bex? Because without Dad ever having to say, I know that talking about Mum being dead makes him sad all over again, and I usually try to avoid that if I can. But I went ahead anyway, because I really needed to know what he thought. If Dad said we ought to stop Eric thinking what he did, we'd have to start work right away. Eric can be very stubborn, and once he's on a roll with something it can take a while to wear him down. I should know – I'm the one who finally got him to eat apples with the peel on, and drink orange juice with bits in it, and that took *months*.

But Dad kind of dismissed it all. That should have been a relief to me, although as it happens it wasn't, but I'll explain why not in a minute.

'It's just Dragon Boy spinning over the top again, Lizzie love,' he said. 'Nothing new there, and nothing to worry about. Like the dinosaur craze, and Spiderman, and dragons too, although I admit *that's* gone on longer than I expected. But you know how he gets fixed on something and won't let go? This is just another phase of it. He gets an idea in his head and he grabs it and runs with it, and then – *poof!* It's over. But while he's on it, nothing distracts him.'

Dad ran his hand through his hair distractedly, and then grinned at me. 'There's an old poem about this, you know,' Dad said. 'Your mum would have remembered it straight away and I bet she'd have known it off by heart, too. It starts with something about, "*If you can keep your head…*"' And he nodded and muttered to himself under his breath for a minute or two, trying to bring the poem into his head so he could say it for me, but in the end he shrugged, and gave up. 'I can't do it all, Lizzie, in fact I can't do much of it! I'll just recite the bits I can remember.' Then Dad stood up and threw out his arms in a big gesture, like he was a comic actor playing around. He struck a pose, and started reciting:

'*If you can keep your head when all about you
Are losing theirs, and blaming it on you.
If you can* – um, dah dah dah – *when all around
are doubting you…*'

Then he paused, and went back to being Dad instead of being a hammy actor. 'And *here's* the bit that made me think of Eric!' he added, grinning triumphantly, and he started declaiming again:

'If you can wait and not be tired by waiting...
Oh, and this bit, too:
If you can hold on, when there's nothing in you
Except the will that says to you: "Hold on!"'

Dad thumped his chest dramatically, struck another final pose, and then flopped back into his chair. I didn't really get what he was on about; he hadn't actually explained the point of the poem.

'Yeah, well, but if *what*, Dad? If you could, then – what would happen?'

Dad struck his hand across his forehead in another hammy gesture, and laughed. 'Oh, right! If *what*, indeed, young Lizzie! The poem's *called* "If", you see, and what it's saying is that if you could do all those things – be brave and honest and persistent, plus all the other things I can't remember – then *"Yours is the Earth and everything that's in it"*, according to the poet.'

'So...do you think Eric could have the whole Earth, just for being *stubborn*?' I asked. I still didn't get it. It sounded mad to me, like Bex's looking on the bright side gone way overboard – but here's what I worked out later on. You probably think the poem's silly; I know I did. But I found out it was written almost a hundred years ago, and people believed that whole thing about perseverance then, like Dad said. It'd be like how we go on these days about finding your true destiny, which shows how much things change. On the other hand, maybe the perseverance thing's still true. Maybe you *can* get what you want if you just stick at it for long enough and don't let other people put you off. I wish I was sure of myself, like Eric is, because I tend to be more of a 'whatever the last person said' thinker, and I know how pathetic that is. Even Susie gets frustrated with me doing it, and she's a friend.

After he'd acted out the poem, Dad got back to Eric. 'Remember about Transformers?' he said. 'Remember how Eric's been with every single thing he's ever got his teeth into, up to and including now?' And I did remember, all too well. And yet...and yet, this didn't seem exactly the same to me. I heard Eric again in my head, saying: 'But you weren't there. You didn't see her.' I thought: *Eric does think he really did see her. It isn't one of his games. He believes it.* I hadn't seen the person Eric saw; the person I knew wasn't Mum – who couldn't possibly be Mum. Dad hadn't heard Eric tell the story, and he hadn't heard the confident certainty in Eric's voice. But I didn't see how I could explain that to Dad. If I tried, I'd have to pay more attention to that panicky thump I'd felt in my heart when Eric had told me, and I didn't want to.

Bex took the same line as Dad. 'Just let it play itself out, Princess,' she advised. 'He'll forget what he saw and what he said about it, or he'll turn it into a whole new game, or whatever. He's best left alone when he's like this; you don't want to make too much of it or it'll just bring out his stubborn side, and then there's a new problem to deal with. Trust me, let it be.'

Well, OK, is what I thought. *We'll give it a try.*

So that's what we all did. It didn't actually work, but it took me a while to see that it wasn't working – and what's more, that it never would. Not in a million years. Not on Eric. I think I knew that all along, in my heart. But I wasn't listening to my heart at the time, or it would have told me that ignoring it – pretending Eric hadn't said what he said, or didn't mean it even if he had said it – was a dumb idea.

For a couple of days, Eric nagged me about it. 'Can we phone the museum today, Lizzie, and talk to Mum?' he'd say. 'Or you could write to her there and put our whole address at the top, with our phone number, and she could call us when she's not too busy.'

I didn't cope very well. I'd just say things like, 'We'll just have to wait and see,' or, 'But right now, let's stack the dishwasher,' or, 'Well, we could think about that, but have you done your homework?' I know how lame I sounded; I embarrassed myself, and I know that I confused Eric.

He gave up on me after a while and started on Bex. Did she know he'd seen our mum? Wouldn't Bex like to meet her? Bex coped better than me, even though she was floundering around too. Her technique was to talk to Eric about seeing Mum, and then sort of lead him on to talking about other things – other imaginary things, like she thought the Mum-sighting really was. I admired that; it was subtle but the message was clear too: *all* these things are in your imagination, Eric. But he didn't fall for that either. I never heard him trying the story out on Dad: he probably realised he wouldn't get a sympathetic hearing.

I know now that I should have stuck to my guns from the start, because pretending that what he'd said wasn't real just made Eric worse. What Bex had been worried about – his stubbornness – came out anyway, and ignoring his story didn't soothe him at all. Eric was used to everyone joining in his games, especially me. And when we played them, I'd always behaved like I believed in them as much as he did. So did Bex, for that matter. Even Dad, to a certain extent. Eric took it on trust that we'd do that every time, so it was confusing for him when, all of a sudden, we weren't going along with him any more. He must have felt like the boy who cried 'Wolf!' when there wasn't really a wolf around, so people stopped believing him – and when there was a real wolf, no one came to help.

Instead of putting him off like it was meant to, ignoring it made Eric turn in on himself and his imaginative powers. He talked to himself even more than before. He talked to the memory box in the mornings and after school as well as at bedtime; and he talked a lot to Mum, too, right out loud. That really stuck out – the talking to Mum bit – because he wasn't talking as much to me or Bex or Dad any more.

Lots of people don't think little kids understand what adults are thinking or doing. Sometimes they – the adults, I mean – behave as if children are deaf and can't hear what's being said right in front of them. But none of that is true: they *do* understand, and even if they don't know what the words mean, they can feel the emotions behind the words. It's funny how adults behave as if they've forgotten that as soon as they grow up; it's like losing a whole room full of memories and then pretending you never had them in the first place.

I could tell Eric knew perfectly well what was going on – that we were all *pretending* not to take any notice of his story about Mum. And in return, Eric was *pretending* that our opinions didn't matter to him, not one scrap. He'd just carry on anyway. So what we were doing – although we'd meant it to have the opposite effect – was encouraging his stubborn streak to thrive and grow. It was rather ironic, really. And after a while I didn't just feel sorry for Eric, I also admired his persistence.

Dad just kept saying we should hang on tight, and Eric would come round. Bex was out of her depth, like I was, although she was doing her level best to cope. I didn't blame her for toeing Dad's line and waiting for the bright side to show itself. But I decided to try another strategy, and maybe that shows I was finally standing up for my own opinions about something important, like Susie says I should. I didn't think that at the time, though: all I thought about was what would be best for Eric.

I'd tried to figure out how to help him admit the truth about what he'd seen, but it was a bit late now to go back to, *No, you didn't see Mum.* So I wondered about going back to the museum, and having another look at this not-Mum person. When Eric saw her again, he'd have to admit it wasn't Mum at all – just someone who looked similar, probably with the same colour hair, like mine. Dad calls it chestnut, like a pony, but it's red in sunlight and Mum called it red, too. She said it was a sign of having a hot temper, but I don't think she had one and I don't seem to have one either. It takes me ages to get really cross about something, and even then I don't do much shouting or carrying on – not like Eric. He's got a hot temper all right, although he doesn't have red hair; his is like Dad's, dark and curly.

Anyway, I thought the return-visit plan could work – because no way was I admitting that Eric actually could have seen Mum. I couldn't. Not at that stage. And it really was a crazy idea. So the next time Eric mentioned Mum, I took him up on it. He'd been doing a lot of virtual phone chats, and I felt very uncomfortable about them. He'd say something, and then he'd wait with his head cocked, like he was listening to what she said back. Then he'd nod, and say something in reply to what he'd heard – well, what he imagined he'd heard, anyway.

You mightn't think it was very different from other things that Eric did, and maybe it wasn't. Lots of kids do weird stuff for a while; Susie once told me that Mia had an imaginary friend she talked to for a whole year, just before she started school. Susie said that after a while the whole family started talking to Mimbo – Mimbo was Mia's friend's name. Mia was delighted when the rest of them joined in and it stopped her getting upset when someone sat on him – or anyway, when they sat down where she said he was – because now they checked first. And they asked him things like, was he comfortable on the ledge at the back of the car, and had he had enough juice at mealtimes, or was he was tired and did he want to go to bed now? That sort of thing. But I didn't fancy doing that for Eric. Anyway, there he was carrying an imaginary conversation with imaginary Mum about the dragon chain, so it was an ideal moment to say something distracting.

'Would you like to go back to the museum, Eric?' I asked casually. 'We could maybe go together, just you and me? You can wear the chain if you like; no one there will mind.' You'll notice what I didn't say to him, though. I didn't say, *Would you like to go back and have another look at Mum in the gift shop? Maybe have a little chat with her about the dragon chain while you're there?* I couldn't have got the words out, but it didn't matter: Eric knew perfectly well what I meant. And my timing was good, too.

The school holidays started the week after, and Dad had agreed that we could go off together in the daytime. And it's easy to get to the museum; I'd done it before. A bus down to Selfridges in Oxford Street and then another one to Cromwell Road, and you're there.

Eric beamed at me. He looked so relieved, like he'd finally got the attention he needed, and I really felt for him at that moment.

'Yes please, Princess Lizzie,' he said. 'That would be bonza.' Bonza is one of Bex's words. It might be Australian slang or it might be one she's made up; I don't know which, but either way it means something's ace.

'You're on!' I said. We high-fived each other, and then Eric gave me an enormous hug, like he was truly grateful that I was helping him. That night, at bedtime, he asked me to do the spell for him, and when we got to the end he made up different words quietly to himself, although not so quietly that I couldn't hear what he said:

Two tales for a dragon chain
One spell for finding Mum.

He looked angelically sweet as he snuggled down in his bed, and I thought I was doing the right thing at last. I still worried about it though, because what if my idea was too harsh? Taking him back to the museum just to show him he was wrong – making it impossible for him to keep up the fantasy. How would he be when he had to give up the whole idea? I wished he'd got hooked on something else. I wished he'd seen the Tooth Fairy come to life in the museum gift shop. I'd rather he'd invented almost anything else than Mum coming back from the dead. But he had no idea how confused and miserable I felt about that, and I couldn't explain it to him. I just hoped it would all go away.

If Eric *still* didn't give it up after we'd been back to the gift shop, I'd have to talk to Dad and Bex again. I'd try to make them see how far Eric had gone down the road of believing in what he said. I thought if I could make them see that, they'd understand that Dad's plan wasn't the right one for him. Maybe they'd even see that I knew Eric better than they did. Which was something I was only just beginning to understand myself.

8

We'd been to the Natural History Museum when Eric was five. Eric was majorly excited, and once he saw the prehistoric things at the museum he dropped his other passions and concentrated on dinosaurs. Especially diplodocus because of the enormous skeleton in the entrance hall, which stunned him into silence the moment he saw it.

But going again this time, just the two of us, was different. I didn't know how he'd react when he *didn't* see Mum in the gift shop, and I knew that if he threw a tantrum about it, I mightn't be able to stop him. One time last year we were in a supermarket with Dad, and he had to carry Eric outside kicking and screaming. I knew I couldn't manage that by myself.

I thought Eric was anxious, too. Not because of maybe having a tantrum; he doesn't shame that easily. But if he really and truly thought he'd seen Mum, then he'd be wishing and hoping to see her again. I didn't know how he'd feel when he couldn't hang on to that any longer.

Bex knew where we were going, but I hadn't told Dad because he'd decided to ignore Eric, and I was doing the exact opposite. Bex knew I hadn't said anything to him, and she knew why not, too. Bex sometimes seems just a cheerful and positive person, with everything about her up front where you can see it. But in fact behind all the fun and games she's thoughtful, and she thinks I need to stand up for myself more, like Susie says. And when I told Bex where we were going all she said was, did we want to take a picnic lunch to eat in Regent's Park on the way home? Which we did, of course.

'You're on holiday, Princess,' she said when we left. 'Make the most of it while it's not raining. It won't last long.'

'Which won't?' I asked. 'The not raining, or the holiday?'

'Both. Either. Go on now, the pair of you!'

Eric was in a very good mood, and he even got me to help with a sandwich hug for Bex before we went – which is where you hug someone, one from each side, so they're in the middle like the filling in a sandwich. We usually do it to Dad when we're being the all-for-one-and-one-for-all-ers, but we did a special one on Bex this time, and you could tell she liked it. So we went off to catch the bus in good moods, which lasted even after we arrived and saw hundreds of people already in the queue, shuffling slowly up the museum steps to the big front doors. We weren't the only people who thought the museum would be fun to go to in the school holidays.

Eric usually hates waiting for anything, but he stayed cheerful, and he didn't complain about the queue, which he usually would. We played 'I Spy' for a while, and then he invented a game on the spot to count up everyone wearing pink. There were a surprising lot of them if you included spots and stripes and T-shirts as well as scarves and socks, and he didn't even mind when I won with the bobble on a baby's hat. So it didn't seem to take long to get to the head of the queue, and then through the security check. And then there we were, inside the main hall, right under the diplodocus's chin.

I'd never gone into a museum and turned straight away into the gift shop, but that's what Eric and I did without even discussing it. Everyone else was racing into another long queue, the one for Mythical Creatures, so we more or less had the shop to ourselves.

It's got good things in it, the Natural History Museum gift shop. Like the elephant poo paper that Eric loves, and lollipops with things like 'Extinction Sucks' on them, and jelly moulds in the shape of human brains. Of course, this time we weren't interested in buying anything so we stopped just inside the entrance to check things out. I saw straight away that there was more than one counter, which slightly complicated the job. Also, you can't see all the counters from one spot – you have to move around to find them, one by one. But Eric didn't seem bothered by any of that. He walked off confidently down the shop, but stopped before he'd got past the 'Grow Your Own Crystals' display, and rushed back again.

'Help me, Lizzie, it's stuck!' he hissed frantically, tugging at the neck of his top. Then he was off again, with the dragon chain on display, but I stayed where I was. I wasn't sure what to do. Should I follow Eric around to see that he didn't do anything outrageous? Or should I do my own looking?

I decided on a combination. I wandered through the shop, scoping out all the female grown-ups, and keeping an ear and an eye out for Eric. Checking out the people didn't take that long. There were two young men behind one of the counters, and a teenage girl with a nose ring at another one. At the third counter was a woman about Mrs Oliver's age, with glasses and blonde hair. No one who looked anything like Mum.

Eric found me again, over by the jelly moulds. 'She isn't here today,' he said. 'I can't see her at all.' He looked disappointed, but not exactly devastated. I wondered what he thought about *not* finding her – whether he still thought she'd actually existed. He could tell what I was thinking. 'She *was*, Lizzie,' he said earnestly. 'She really was, she's just not here at this exact minute. Maybe...maybe she's having a coffee break.'

But that exact minute was when I started to feel cross. Frankly, a hiccup like this hadn't been part of my plan. I'd thought there'd be someone who looked a bit like Mum, and Eric would have to admit it wasn't her, and then we could go to the Mythical Creatures exhibition and enjoy ourselves. The hard part should be over by now, and we should have started getting back to normal. It was frustrating and irritating to have my plans dashed.

'And exactly how long do you want to wait to see if she comes back again?' I asked. I probably sounded snappy; I certainly felt it.

Eric stared at me. 'It's my *mother* we're talking about, you know,' he said, raising his voice slightly.

'And yours too, Lizzie, don't forget.' He sounded like a reasonable adult explaining something to a sulky child. 'Don't you want to see her too?'

No, I thought. *No, Eric, I don't actually want to see her at all, thanks.* But I didn't say that out loud. Instead, like so often, I gave in. 'OK, let's give it – say, half an hour,' I suggested. 'That's longer than a coffee break. OK? Then we'll come back and look again.'

So back we went, out into the entrance hall, to line up for Mythical Creatures tickets. The queue had cleared so we didn't have to wait long, and I got timed tickets for 11.15. That gave us about forty-five minutes to wait, so we went up the grand staircase to the first gallery, which I thought would keep Eric entertained for a while. It didn't work, though. He kept grabbing my wrist to look at my watch and check how much time had passed, and peering down into the main hall to see if his mystery woman was anywhere around. It drove me mad, but I gritted my teeth and stuck it out until our time was up and we could go back downstairs. Then we went back into the gift shop. And Eric's mystery woman still wasn't there.

By then I'd had more than enough of being kind and understanding. I was sick of trying to help Eric come to terms with what was true and what wasn't.

I didn't even care about being mean; I'd had more than enough. I felt resentful, which isn't something I'd usually admit to. You might expect that I'd often feel resentful with Eric – playing his games and entertaining him and worrying about him: all that. But I'd never felt like this before, and then all of a sudden I did. I was itchy with resentment and irritation. I didn't want to put up with another minute of it. I was finally beginning to assert myself, like a worm turning at the very last moment. *We could stand here all day, waiting for someone who doesn't exist to turn up*, I thought. *What'll I do then, for pity's sake?*

So I was all for giving up, and going over to the Mythical Creatures entrance in case they'd let us in early. Trying to get Eric to agree to that, though, was a challenge. He looked at me in amazement when I suggested giving up, like I'd gone majorly doolally. I took his shoulder and tried to turn him towards the door, but he shook my hand off like an irritating fly. Then he marched determinedly over to the counter where the older woman in glasses was serving people. I saw him put his sweetest expression on his face as he went, too – the one that Mrs Oliver says is his 'charming the socks off snakes' face. I could tell it worked on this woman, as well as on snakes. As soon as she'd finished with her other customers she bent forward over the counter to Eric, and smiled encouragingly at him.

He smiled back. 'I was in here with my class before the holidays started,' he announced.

The woman nodded. 'That's right, dear,' she said. 'Lots of school parties came to see the Mythical Creatures show. Did you come to see it again today?'

I hoped very much that Eric wouldn't say, *No, I came to see my mother*, because of the extra explaining that would involve. But I needn't have worried.

'I came back to talk to the nice lady who was here. In here, in the shop,' he explained. 'I want to show her my dragon chain.' And then he gave the woman one of his most dazzling smiles and said, 'I don't mean *you* aren't nice too, you know.'

She laughed. 'That's very kind of you, young man,' she said. 'But I don't know who you mean. Which other lady?' She gestured towards the teenage girl at the next counter, but Eric shook his head firmly.

'No. She has red hair.' He looked at her hopefully, waiting, and I held my breath. I knew she'd say something like, *Who? No one here has red hair*, or even just, *There aren't any more staff in the gift shop*, and then I'd have to get Eric away before his weird story started tumbling out...

'Ah,' said the woman thoughtfully. 'You must mean Eliza. Younger than me? And older than her?' She gestured again at the teenager. 'With reddish hair?' she added. 'A bit like your sister's, actually,' she went on obligingly, pointing at me and then smiling at Eric again.

Eric's face lit up like the morning sun. 'She's called *Eliza*?' he said excitedly. 'My *sister's* called Eliza, too!' But the next moment his face fell as he remembered that Mum's first name was Alice, and not the same as mine at all.

The woman didn't notice his change of expression. 'Well, *there's* a coincidence,' she said happily. 'Eliza's rather an unusual name.'

And it was while they were chatting away that a sliver of ice slid into my heart. I stopped hearing what the two of them were saying, like being in a goldfish bowl and watching people outside open and shut their mouths but not being able to hear what they're saying. Or inside my head the confusion was maybe more like a slot machine – you know how there's a display with a row of pictures on it, and you put money in and pull a lever, and the rows of pictures all whizz round clicking away, and when they stop you get a whole new line of pictures? And if the pictures match, you've won? Well, it was like that. Everything I had been certain about – the pictures I'd had in my head about Eric's story – all whizzed around, but when they stopped – *ker-ching!* – the pictures looked completely and utterly different.

Because it's true that Eliza isn't Mum's name: it's just the name she chose for me. But the thing is, *I know why she called me Eliza.* I still remember exactly what she told me because I felt so proud of the reason. It was like a secret between us. Mum said, 'I called you Eliza because it's always been my favourite name in the whole world. When I was little I wanted to be called Eliza instead of Alice, and I pretended it was my own secret name: *Eliza Brown.*'

She said it almost like it was a spell, sort of quiet and thoughtful, and she didn't say anything else for a minute or two. She even looked a little bit sad, which is slightly strange because I wouldn't have thought that a name would matter all that much. But then she smiled at me again and said, 'That's why I called *you* Eliza, Lizzie love. Because for me it's the prettiest name in the whole world. And if I ever have another life, I'll call myself Eliza, too!'

She laughed about that, like she'd said something very silly – and I laughed too because when you're little you'd never imagine that your mother could have another life. But now that I'm older, I know they can. On TV a while ago I saw a programme about a woman who'd run away from her home and her children. And she changed her name, and started a whole new life with a new name and everything.

I shook myself. This was crazy. Mum was dead. I *knew* she was dead.

But what if she isn't? The little doubting voice started up in my head again. *What if she isn't dead at all? What if instead, she secretly ran away and started a new life?* And called herself Eliza, like I suddenly knew she would have done.

Everything I'd ever known about Mum suddenly turned upside down in my head. I don't know how long I stood there, but it can't have been more than a couple of minutes. Then Eric was back beside me, tugging at my arm.

'Lizzie!' he said. 'Listen! That nice woman says that Mum isn't working here, but she *was*! She was when I was here before! She might come back! So I was right, wasn't I?' Then his face clouded over. 'Except... Why would Mum change her name?' he whispered. 'Why would she call herself Eliza?'

I knew just how he felt.

'Let's go and see the Mythical Creatures now,' I said, taking his hand. 'And we'll talk about everything afterwards, OK?' And for once, he didn't resist.

9

I didn't expect to, but we had a great time in the exhibition. There's something called the eye of the storm, which happens in the middle of a hurricane when the wind stops shrieking and battering everything in its path, and goes quiet and still. That's where Eric and I were, in the eye of the storm. We hadn't got to the bit where all the shrieking and battering started up again, although I knew we would, but I put that out of my mind to worry about later.

So we giggled and gasped our way around the exhibition. Eric loved knowing more about them all than I did, because of having seen it before. He could explain things to me, like hippogriffs and krakens. He could act superior when I was surprised by something like the roc, which turned out to have surprised even Marco Polo, so I didn't feel too much of a fool. Marco Polo said that the roc could seize an elephant in its talons and carry it high into the air, and then drop it so that the elephant smashed to pieces. Yuck!

And when we came to the end of all the displays there was an activity room, where you could play on computers and test your knowledge, and make your own virtual creatures on the screens. I loved it all, I honestly did. It felt like the old days for both of us.

When we'd finally had enough we left and caught a bus back to Oxford Street. Normally we'd have changed buses there and got another one to Camden, but it was my turn not to want to hang about, so we set off to walk up to Regent's Park. Bex says that walking fast helps her to think, and we walked fast because it wasn't warm, and because we had such a lot whirling around our brains. Eric is one of the fastest runners in his year, but walking's different, and I walked so fast up the street he had to trot to keep up with me. I think my stamina was improving because I didn't get puffed, even though I was carrying our lunch in my backpack. Eric didn't mind being hurried; he was too busy talking non-stop about did I think a Chinese dragon was better than a griffin, and would a yowie beat a yeti or a bigfoot?

He was still going nineteen to the dozen, as

Mrs Oliver says, when we reached Hanover Gate, just before you get to the mosque. Normally we'd have gone further up the road because there's a statue of Saint George and the Dragon in the middle of the next roundabout and Eric always likes to look at it. But today I put food ahead of the dragon statue, and Eric agreed, so we turned into the park.

'You know what, Lizzie?' Eric said as we walked up beside the mosque, and then waited to cross into the park. 'This is my best day ever!' His face was lit up and glowing with excitement. 'I mean it,' he went on. 'Really and truly, the best ever.' And he reached out and patted my arm, like he really *did* mean it and he wanted to say thank you. I've said it before: Eric can be very sweet. I didn't feel cross or fed up with him any more; I think the fast walking had shaken my bad mood underground.

I was back to thinking how much I wanted to protect him, not upset him. I didn't want him to go on thinking he'd seen Mum, and although the creepy bit about the mystery woman's name had shaken me up, I still couldn't honestly believe it. How could I? But I didn't want him to be disappointed either, and I didn't want to see his face fall as the truth sunk in. Still, I'd made up my mind to be straight with him. *One more try* is what I decided, like making myself a promise.

So that was my new plan.

As soon as you get into the park from Hanover Gate there's a playground on the left and a little boating pool on the right. Lots of people don't go any further into the park than that, which is a bit of a waste considering how big the park is and how many other attractions there are. It's rather like how people cluster at the front of a bus after they've got on, instead of moving down and finding some space.

I know the Hanover Gate part because Dad used to walk us across there before Eric started school. It's a nice walk, and there were always other little kids there for him to play with. Eric still casts a longing glance at the playground and the pedal boats when we come this way, but you can't stay there to eat your lunch. There are too many geese and ducks hanging around, pigeons too, and they all beg for food and make your life a misery if they so much as hear a paper bag rustle. So we went further on.

As soon as you cross the first Hanover Bridge it's a lot calmer and quieter, and when you cross the second one you're in a different bit of the park with big playing fields, and not so many people. We know this part well because it's close to where we live, and by then I'd decided exactly where to go. If you walk around the curve of the big lake there's a grassy place that slopes down to the water. There are benches and even a lifejacket on a stand in case you ever happen to see someone who's fallen into the water. In the past, Eric and I always argued about which of us would throw the lifejacket and which of us would run for help, although it was usually me to throw and Eric to run, because he's the speedy one. But we weren't going to discuss that today.

So anyway, that's where I'd decided we should sit and eat. There aren't many ducks and geese there, and no pigeons at all – all the birds tend to stick to places where there are lots of people to hassle for food. Dad says birds have tiny brains, but I wonder about that; they're so smart about finding food and so persistent when they do. We chose the bench by the big willow tree because you can look out over the lake and admire the view, and watch for anyone in danger of drowning. Then I opened my backpack and got out Bex's picnic lunch. I knew it would be good, and it was: she'd really gone to town, as Mrs Oliver would say, with a celebration holiday picnic. She'd made us cheese and veggie empanadas from scratch, which were totally delicious, and she'd given us little tubs of spicy dip for them. One of the dips didn't have coriander in it because she'd even remembered I hate coriander. Plus there were tiny tomatoes and baby carrots to eat whole, and enough flapjacks and fruit juice for afters.

By then Eric and I were back in our old routines with each other, and everything was fine while we ate. We even had a short competition to think of the best word to describe Bex's lunch, which we hadn't done for ages – bonza, major, ace and awesome were all up there, but bonza won in the end.

'I love Bexie, don't you? She's bonza, too,' said Eric through a mouthful of flapjack, eyeing mine as well. He always wants to start a meal with dessert and work backwards, and on a picnic what's to stop you?

I narrowed my eyes at him and put on Mrs Oliver's voice, the stern one she uses if she thinks we've gone too far. '*Bexie?*' I said. 'Who's this Bex or Bexie person when she's at home? It's Rebecca to you, young fella-me-lad, and don't forget your manners.' I got Mrs Oliver's voice exactly right, and Eric laughed so much he fell off the bench and forgot about stealing my flapjacks.

After we'd finished eating we just sat peacefully for a while. I always enjoy watching other people and trying to guess things about their lives – it's like looking at people on trains from my bedroom window, and no one could see my brain spinning around trying to sort things out. Even Eric was relaxed, and he hummed the fox song to himself while he packed up our lunch rubbish without me even asking him to do it.

But then he turned to me, suddenly serious again. 'You do believe me now, don't you Lizzie?' He gazed at me intently, and I noticed he was starting to look like Dad. Already he had the same way of frowning when he concentrated, so that his eyebrows tilted up at the ends. I took a breath and let it out slowly, like Bex says helps you to stay calm.

'It's not about believing you, or not believing you,' I said. 'Mum's dead, Eric, so whoever you saw, it can't have been her.' But the moment I'd said that I started to relent. I knew I couldn't leave it like that, and anyway there was the whole bit about the name that bothered me... So I tried again. 'Well, OK, I see why you might think...' But my voice trailed off once more.

He's only seven, I said to myself. I didn't know how to begin to explain what I thought. I put my head back and stared up at a flock of starlings that was wheeling around over the lake. The birds shifted and parted and shifted again against the pale sky, while I tried to sort through the swirl of thoughts in my head. Eric was still staring at me with a frown of concentration. Then he said, 'But it just about *could* be true? Is that what you think?'

I nodded cautiously. 'In another world, it might be true,' I said slowly. 'But if it *was* true, if Mum was alive and not dead after all, it would mean a whole lot of other things had gone wrong. A whole lot of things we trust – well, they'd turn out to be lies. And I don't want – I don't think we should want that.'

I had to try to be honest – with myself and with Eric. As honest as I knew how. 'I don't think you understand what it would mean,' I went on. 'And it's crazy even to think it. Do you realise that?' I waited until Eric nodded reluctantly and then I took another deep breath.

'Mum's dead,' I said. 'She's been dead for almost five years. People don't just stop being dead and start being alive: not in the real world. They might in stories, though,' I admitted, while I tried to remember if any stories Eric knew might include that happening. Maybe some fairy stories *were* like that –

'But if you see her, and it's really her, then she's not dead after all,' Eric pointed out. He was trying to be logical about it.

'OK, yes, that'd be true,' I agreed. 'But we don't know that it was Mum you saw, not for sure.' I looked at him carefully. 'I don't think you were really, truly, absolutely, one hundred per cent sure that it was Mum you saw. Be honest.'

Eric hesitated so long that I thought he was going to hold out on me, or go back to being stubborn. But in the end he reluctantly nodded his head. 'That's why I wanted to look at her again, when I went back into the shop after lunch,' he admitted. 'To be sure. But it was *daytime*, and it was *Mum*. It wasn't like looking for the foxes when it's got dark and anyway they're hiding.'

'So...' I paused, and then started again. 'So, if we're going to find out the truth, we need a plan. Have you got one?' That was mean of me really; I knew he wouldn't have a plan. But I didn't have one of my own, either, at that stage.

'We could ask Dad why he thinks Mum's dead,' Eric suggested, looking doubtful even as he said it, but I shook my head firmly at him.

'We can't ask him, it wouldn't be fair,' I said, and Eric nodded; he knew about Dad not wanting to talk about Mum. I didn't want to mention any other reasons to Eric, even though I was trying to be truthful. I just couldn't. I'd have to say something like, *Dad might know she's not really dead. He might be keeping the truth from us*, and I didn't want Eric to even think of that.

I couldn't actually believe that Dad would tell us

such a massive lie, but if you didn't know Dad like I do, you'd have to admit it was a possible explanation. So it was like my head was saying, *You have to admit, it's an explanation*, while my heart was saying, *Dad wouldn't lie to me: not about that.*

If Eric *hadn't* gone to the museum when he did, and if he hadn't seen – well, whoever he saw – someone he thought was Mum, and if he wasn't so convinced that the person was Mum, then the idea of Dad lying to us about her all these years would never, ever have come up. I was sorry that it had; it felt like I was betraying him even though I'd only thought it and I hadn't said it out loud. But I knew that letting Eric suspect it wasn't on.

So I said it firmly again: we couldn't ask Dad, so we'd have to think about what to do, and come up with a decent plan. I did think, but I didn't say, that maybe we'd have to go back to the museum *again*, and see if the mystery woman had really left for good. Maybe she'd only gone on leave and she'd be back again. Maybe we could talk to a different person at the museum, and they might know where she'd gone and how we could find her. But at the same time, I had my doubts about doing that. In my experience, adults don't want to tell someone my age anything that's a bit confidential, and asking those questions would seem unusual. And I was puzzled about how to get around that problem, until I remembered there *was* a grown-up I could talk to. One I could trust.

Bex.

10

'So it's not just Eric who's turning into a bit of a fruit-loop,' Bex said, grinning at me sympathetically. 'It's both of you now, is it?'

I'd explained what happened at the museum, and what Eric and I had talked about in the park. I hadn't told her everything by any means, like I hadn't mentioned how weird I felt about this mystery woman's name being the same as mine. But it had been enough to get Bex on my side.

Bex reached over the kitchen table and patted my hand comfortingly, like she'd read my mind and knew how I was feeling. Then she sat down and pushed a tray of flapjacks across the table to me. I love them when they're just out of the oven and still sticky-soft, and Bex knows that. She watched while I ate two of them straight away, and while I licked my fingers to pick up the last crumbs. She handed me a piece of kitchen towel to wipe my hands on, still silent. Then finally she nodded her head sharply, like she'd come to a decision, and leaned back in her chair.

'You were right all along, Princess,' she said. 'I know you had your own ideas about dealing with Eric, and he's been a whole lot better since you said you'd take him back to the museum – so well done you.' She grinned at me, and I felt great.

'But it still needs sorting out, once and for all,' Bex went on. 'And without upsetting your dad, if we can avoid that. Plus he's been so keen on ignoring it, it'll be hard to shift him.'

'Sounds like Eric,' I said, and Bex smiled. 'Like father, like son, eh?' Then she frowned. 'One thing though – there's no other family you can talk to about this, is there? No old auntie or granny somewhere to help sort it out?'

I shook my head. Most people have someone like that, but I knew we didn't have aunts or uncles or grandparents. Mum and Dad had friends who used to come round for barbecues in our garden when we were in Cambridge, but I don't even know what happened to them. We don't get Christmas cards from them and I expect that's because Dad never said where we were going. We just upped and left.

Bex nodded. 'OK then, we're on our own here,'

she said. 'Not such a bad thing, either, we can do it our way – as soon as we work that out.' Her positive spin made me feel encouraged, even though I suspected she felt as confused as I did: she just hid it better.

'So,' she said briskly, 'there are two parts to this puzzle, right?' I nodded although I didn't know what the two parts were; I just wanted her to go on talking. Which she did.

'One part's Eric,' she said, 'and the other part is, who on earth can this Eliza person be? She's probably no one, but we have to be sure of that – we have to lay the ghost.'

A ghost? I stared at Bex in dismay for a couple of seconds until I realised she didn't mean that not-Mum was actually a ghost, it was just a way of saying, *We have to sort it out properly before it haunts our lives.* And I agreed with that. But just when I was feeling comforted and happily waiting for her to sort the problems out, Bex surprised me all over again. She looked straight at me, and narrowed her eyes in a kind of, *this is what I have to say to you* way, and she said, very seriously: 'And in answer to something that might be worrying you: *no way.*'

I sat and gawped at her, and my mouth probably dropped open too. And while my brain was still struggling to understand she added, 'He wouldn't.

He just wouldn't!' Which made it, as I said later, about as clear as mud. Then she slapped the tabletop for emphasis, and said again firmly, 'Absolutely not. Not your dad.' So then I finally got it. Bex had skipped a stage of explaining and gone straight for one of the things that was worrying me the most; something I hadn't even mentioned to her. She understood anyway, which was a real comfort. And I knew she was right, and it's what I'd thought myself, but I needed someone else to agree with me. My dad, he's not perfect or anything, but he wouldn't lie about something as big as this.

'I'm sure it's not your mum, you know,' Bex went on after we'd sorted that out. 'But even supposing just for a moment that your mum's somehow still alive, then your dad couldn't possibly know that himself. He wouldn't hide something that big from you, and anyway, how the heck could he?' She paused for a minute, like I did with Eric when I was trying to work around a tricky thing and say it gently. 'It was a road accident, you know that, don't you?' she said softly. 'Your mum was hit by a car. And if you bear that in mind – plus everything else I've been told – it's not possible that she could still be around and we don't know.'

I nodded. I hadn't been to the funeral – Dad hadn't wanted me to go – but I knew there'd been one and I knew why. Then Bex reached across the table again and stroked my hand comfortingly. 'So it can't be true, sweetie. Although...' She hesitated for a moment. 'Although, maybe a bit of you might *like* it to be true? Is that what's bothering you?' She looked at me, but I looked away. I didn't answer, because I couldn't, not right then. And she didn't nag; she just squeezed my hand and then went on.

'So let's take things one at a time.' Bex held up a hand and then bent one finger down. 'OK, Eric's number one,' she announced, leaning back in her chair. She thought for a minute. 'You know,' she finally said, 'I reckon I can put Eric's main problem in a nutshell. He wants it to be true, what he thinks he saw. So it's like, if he believes it hard enough, then it will be. And *that's* what we have to work on, somehow.' She looked slightly worried about it though, because she knows as well as I do how stubborn Eric can be.

'OK, we'll have to come back to that,' she decided. 'Let's have a go at number two, which is that Eric's mystery woman is apparently one hundred per cent real, but – and this is *so* irritating – she wasn't around when you were there. So Eric couldn't see that she wasn't your mum, which brings us back to problem number one.'

'But the Eliza name thing's sort of funny too, isn't it?' I asked cautiously. I was still curious about that, and the memory of how I'd felt about it kept bothering me.

Bex nodded, and then shrugged. She used her whole body for the shrug, in a kind of mime that said, *What can you do? It happens!* 'Yeah, OK, it's weird all right,' she agreed. 'But that doesn't mean it's not a coincidence. And that's what it is, Lizzie, because it can't be anything else.'

I do see what she means. On the other hand, she might not be so confident if it was *her* name that was the coincidence. It's different when it's that close to you, is all I'm saying.

Bex glanced towards the door to the hall, and lowered her voice a bit. Eric was in his bedroom with Sim, his new friend from school, and they were watching a DVD called *The World's Weirdest Creatures*. There was no chance they'd pay us any attention until it ended, but Bex went to check anyway, just to be safe.

'You know how people say truth is stranger than fiction?' she continued when she came back. 'Well, I reckon that applies here. The woman Eric saw... Obviously, the *truth* is that she looks a bit like your mum. And to make the coincidence even bigger, she's got your name. But that's all. They're both coincidences.' Bex gave a little smile. 'And you know what?' she went on. 'What he saw is someone who looks like *photos* of your mum, which is an entirely different thing. Not everyone looks all that much like their photo. I don't look like my passport photo, for example. At least I hope not; I look terrible in it...mouth like a prune.' She made a prune-shape with her mouth to show me, and I had to smile.

But still, Bex wasn't exactly right about that, because Mum *did* look like her photos. What Dad says is that the camera loved her, and I think that means she never looked awful in a photo, the way some people do – like Bex was saying had happened to her. I look more or less OK in school photos but Mum always looked great in any photo, and basically how she looked in real life is how she looks in the photos we've got.

So I knew that wasn't the problem. The problem was still the same one – that Eric was convinced he'd seen her and needed help to see he must be wrong. And I didn't say it to Bex, but I still thought that he just *might* be right. However crazy that made me. I didn't admit I felt miserable but Bex stayed cheerful and that slightly encouraged me. And although she still couldn't think of the right way to solve the Eric-problem, she promised to think more about it. I did have faith in her, but to be honest I didn't rate her chances very highly.

'One other thing, sweetie,' she added, getting up from the table to start dinner. She turned away to the cupboards. 'One of us had better have a word with your dad about all this. Maybe you rather than me, do you think?' Then she turned around again, holding a bag of potatoes, and saw my horrified expression.

'Oh, Lizzie! No, I didn't mean that!' She put down the potatoes and held out her hand to me. 'Not that either of us should ask him about your mum again. But he needs to know Eric's taken a few more steps down this rocky old road of his, and that we need to find the right way to reel him back in.' She looked at me again thoughtfully, and then turned and started scrubbing the potatoes at the sink.

'Do you want me to tell him for you?' she asked, but I didn't think that would work. I wasn't frightened of talking to Dad about it; I just didn't want to, especially now I thought he'd been wrong about dealing with Eric right from the start. But I still thought it was my job, because it was slightly my fault that Eric was still so fixed on the whole idea.

'Could you be there when I tell him?' I suggested.

'You could help if I get in a muddle. Could you stay on tonight after dinner?' Bex said she'd gladly do that, and that now I wasn't to worry any more – I should go and watch something mindless on TV and not even help with the dinner. So I did, and everything felt better, until Dad came home. And even then it was still OK until I actually said... But now I'm running ahead of myself. I want to explain what happened and it's quite hard because it wasn't words that were the problem, it was how Dad *looked*.

Bex said I should wait until Eric was asleep, and I knew it'd be easier without him maybe overhearing something. He was enjoying all the drama a bit much; he *expected* us to be talking about him in hushed voices behind his back, and that wasn't good. Dad was surprised when Bex didn't rush off after dinner, but you could see he was pleased as well. And when he came back into the living room after settling Eric down, Bex said right away, 'Eliza's got something she wants to say.'

It was a helpful prompt, and I liked her using my full name, but of course it meant I couldn't chicken out, or save everything up for another day. So anyway, off I went. I explained how I'd taken Eric back to the museum, and how he'd asked about the woman he'd seen; the one who looked like Mum.

And Dad was looking straight at me and paying full-on attention, which is why suddenly, when I said the next bit, I realised that things weren't OK after all.

I said, 'The thing was, Dad, this woman Eric talked to – she told him her name was Eliza.' And then I corrected myself. 'Not the older woman Eric was talking to – not *her* name. The one who Eric thinks was Mum: she does exist and *her* name's Eliza.'

It took a second for Dad to work out what I meant, but when he did he stopped looking straight at me. He glanced off to the side, and his face changed. It really did: I saw it. It was like something clicked in his mind at that exact moment. He made some connection, and as soon as that happened he needed to hide it from me. Like he was surprised. Like he'd suddenly remembered something he didn't want to be reminded about; something he was going to conceal. And it was only a tiny thing, but that doesn't mean it wasn't real. It was over in a couple of seconds, and if I hadn't been watching him I'd have missed it completely. I didn't know what it all meant, but what I did know was, it meant something to Dad.

I wish now that I'd picked him up about it, but I didn't. I pretended I hadn't seen his face change, just like he pretended that it hadn't. I went on explaining. 'And Eric thought that meant it *was* Mum, because it's my name; he forgot that it wasn't hers.' I paused, and then I added: 'And it was Mum's favourite name, wasn't it?'

Dad was looking at me again by then, although his face was still kind of closed, like he was still trying to hide his feelings. But then he smiled at me, and said softly, 'Well, natch! Of course it was her favourite! It's the name she gave to you, Lizzie.'

I didn't even say what I'd remembered – that it was her favourite name to start with, before I came along, and *that's* why she'd given it to me. And the moment passed, and Bex got in on the conversation, and we talked more about Eric than about Mum or the mystery woman.

But the next day, Bex said straight out that she'd noticed the change in Dad's face, too. She said it before I'd found a way to mention it to her, so it must have been clear, and she must have known I'd noticed. So then I knew I hadn't imagined it.

'He looked like he knew something that he wasn't going to mention, didn't he?' Bex said. 'But you know what, Princess? That'd most likely be because Eliza's *your* name, and so everything's too close for comfort.' She raised her eyebrows, waiting to see if I understood what she meant. And I did, because

I know how protective Dad is with us, so I agreed with her at the time. But when I thought more about it, I wasn't so sure. *Because it had happened again the same night, when we were all still talking.*

I know there could have been a simple reason why Dad hesitated a second time. The conversation had turned mostly into Dad and Bex talking to each other about the problem, and not directly to me any more, which I resented in one way although in another it was a slight relief. And I interrupted them after a while, anyway, because I wanted to get back to what I thought was the main problem: what we could do about Eric's idea. I was saying that the belief had got hold of him so strongly he wasn't going to just give up – we'd have to help him do that. Dad was still saying we should wait him out, and in the end Eric would have to give it up and adjust to reality. Normally I might have agreed with him, even though I thought Dad's idea was too hard on a little boy like Eric. But this time I stayed firm about what I thought, and afterwards I was pleased that I'd stuck to my guns. I pointed out that if anything he'd got *more* determined, not less. We had to show him he was wrong, not just keep telling him he was or ignoring him.

And then suddenly Bex sat up and said, 'You know what, you two? I could try to find out if this

Eliza woman's still working there, at the Natural History Museum. Sometimes a grown-up can ask questions and get better answers than kids are likely to – except for present company, Miss Lizzie, I know you're not a kid any more. Anyway, if she's still there we could try to make Lizzie's idea work one more time.'

And that's when Dad went all peculiar again. His face tightened up and he looked really cross with Bex for suggesting it. Bex couldn't see his face from where she was sitting, but I could, and I was sure he was about to lay down the law and say that Bex couldn't do that. He didn't like the idea one bit.

But then he paused, and shrugged, and ended up more or less agreeing with her. 'Well, OK, why not?' he said. He didn't sound enthusiastic, but he did say it. 'It can't do any harm to prove to Eric this isn't his mother. I'd be inclined to keep on paying it no attention in front of him,' he went on, 'but maybe if this woman is still at the museum, then seeing her again – and seeing that she *isn't* Alice – maybe that'll help him.' And then he sighed and stretched like he was tired, and grinned at me and said, 'Our little Princess Lizzie *never* gave me this kind of trouble when she was Eric's age!'

I had to smile when Bex replied, 'Just you wait till she's a teenager!' Then Bex got her jacket and bag and went home. I went to bed, but I was too edgy to sleep. It would have been easier to ignore those two little moments when Dad looked like he might have a secret, but I couldn't pretend any more. I was majorly certain there was something he was hiding from me; something about Mum. No question. I was so het up about the whole thing now, my head was whirling with all the complications and muddles, and frankly, I hated it all. But I still wanted to try to fix it if I could.

And it's funny – I mean funny-peculiar, not funny-ha-ha – that for a minute or two I was pleased Dad might worry about me instead of Eric. I know that sounds a bit mean, but it's what I felt. Maybe I'm turning into a difficult teenager rather early.

11

After that night I got more anxious about everything, instead of less anxious as I'd been hoping. Eric saying he'd seen Mum had spun all of us way out into the stratosphere, and every time we tried to unspin ourselves something else got sucked in. Bex was doing the least amount of spinning, of course, which made her a comforting person to have around. And I was probably doing the most spinning, which made me feel worse. It was like I was standing on the edge of a cliff and I hadn't realised it was there, and as soon as I'd seen how close the edge was I'd got dizzy with panic, and now I couldn't stop. And I didn't know how to step away from the cliff, either, because at first there was only one barrier between me and safety – what Eric said he'd seen. But now a whole lot more things had clustered around my feet, and they tripped me up every time I tried to move. Even making a list, which can be soothing and help sort out your feelings, made me feel worse when I wrote mine.

Mum was dead, which was bad enough, but I'd learned how to cope with that. Now Mum might not be dead at all, and you'd think that might be a Good Thing to have on a list but it actually felt worse than her being dead.

Next, Mum might have become a ghost, and that's who Eric had seen in the gift shop. But that was such a scary thought, and not helpful or encouraging in any way, so I didn't want to deal with it.

Or, number three, Dad might know something about Mum dying that he'd never told me. Like, that she didn't actually die. And that worry was the main thing keeping me awake at night.

Or even, all of the above.

This was crazy! All of it was crazy! Bex was right; I was turning into a top-notch fruit-loop and I knew I had to stop. But I couldn't put the list items out of my head for long. I couldn't do anything about them myself, I had to wait and see what Bex could find out. And that meant I went straight from being glad it wasn't me who had to do the finding out, to wishing it was me after all just so I could get on with it. I knew she'd do it, but I didn't know when.

In the meantime one thing was a considerable relief to me, and that was Eric being more like the old Eric than the mystery-woman Eric. I don't know why he'd changed, and I didn't ask him in case it started him off again. But he'd eased back on talking to the memory box, and he'd stopped having one-sided conversations with Mum – or if he was still having those, at least he wasn't having them in front of me.

He checked up on things from time to time, though. He'd ask me what was happening about finding Mum, and did I think it would happen soon? But when I told him nothing had happened yet, but that we were on the case, he'd relax again. Just a reality check, is what I thought – more of a fantasy check actually – and all he wanted was to be sure I was still taking him seriously. Once he knew that, he was content again for a while. He wasn't in a completely dragon-free limbo-land – he was still wearing his tail, and putting on his masks, and all that – but we weren't playing the games together any more. He and Sim had worked out some new ones; I think they took turns to be dragons and yetis and yowies. I sort of missed it in a way, but I thought they'd probably need a princess again in a while.

So the two of us put our heads together and worked on a fox chart for Eric's project. We'd decided to rate the foxes by how many times we saw each one on the nights we went along to the bridge to look for them. Every fox-sighting got a square on the chart filled in with a picture of that particular fox, which I drew in pencil and Eric coloured in. We argued a bit about naming each of the foxes, but in the end we went with the names that Eric preferred because, after all, it was his chart. We'd already got Viv and Violet for the two vixens: Viv for White Chin, and Violet for Droopy Ear. I had to agree that they sounded more dignified. And Eric went for Damon for the big dog-fox, because even though we'd never seen him, we knew he must exist.

The two cubs were Camden and Calvin. We didn't know if they were girls or boys so it was fair to have a name for each possibility. Eric got silly and wanted to call them Arthur and Martha because the names rhyme, and anything that does makes him giggle right now: he and Sim are a nightmare when they get started. I talked him out of those because I wanted names that matched their foxy natures. I liked Camden and Calvin Cub, so I told Eric they sounded more scientific.

Eric offered to let me choose any other names we'd need if more foxes turned up, although I didn't think it was likely. Still, I did have names up my sleeve for them: Val for a vixen, Candy and Carlos for cubs, and Dylan for another dog-fox if there happened to be a second one. It was actually fun thinking them up and if we ever have a pet, I'd like to suggest names for it. Not that I think we will: Mrs Oliver has her cat but Dad says it's not right for us because our flat's too small for a cat, and a dog would be even worse because you can't leave them alone – although personally I don't think you should leave a cat alone all day, either. Mrs Oliver's Posh is quite old now but even so, if she's bored, she chews the edges of books so they look like mice have been nibbling at them. Maybe I should just look on the bright side and be glad Eric never wanted to own a spider when he was mad about Spiderman, because I don't like them at all.

When the fox chart was ready, we planned our observations. We decided to watch the foxes whenever we could over the next four weeks, and then record the results. Then we'd do the final chart properly, in colour. I did some quick Aussie knitting in foxy colours so I could decorate the edges with knitted foxes. Dad said he would try to photograph them with the long-distance lens on his camera, and Bex said she'd cook some fox-shaped gingerbread to take into class on project day. It turned into a real team-effort. Dad and Bex were extra-specially keen about helping because they thought it was a distraction from you-know-what, but I knew better than that and I was just helping Eric because I always do.

I was relieved to be comfortable with Eric again, and I just sort of coasted along for a while pretending not to have a list of problems. So when Bex told me one afternoon, completely out of the blue, that she'd finally been to the museum herself and talked to someone in the gift shop, my stomach lurched with dread. I'd put it all so far in the back of my mind I'd been able to forget about it. Well, almost. But, typical Bex, she just came out with it.

'I went to the museum yesterday, Lizzie, and I had a good chat with one of the guys in the gift shop,' is what she said. Just like that, while we were sorting some washing together in the laundry room. Eric was at the park with the other kids from his year, trying out for the football teams, and Dad was so keen on the idea he'd got time off work to go with him. He really wanted Eric to make it and I knew why: he thought it would be an excellent distraction from what he was now calling 'Eric's fancies'. I was glad whether Eric made it or not, because much as I love him it's always nice when he's not around for a while. Also, as I've said before, I like to have time with Bex by myself. I wasn't expecting her to say what she did, though; I'd have liked some warning. Bex folded and stacked pillowcases in the cupboard while she talked, keeping it casual.

'So,' she said briskly, 'this woman, I'm sure she's the one Eric saw. I described her to Mark – he's the guy in the gift shop I chatted to. It wasn't much to go on but Mark knew who I meant straight off. The right age, the right hair, and working in the gift shop just before the school holidays started: it's got to be. Also, Mark said she was only temporary; she wasn't permanent staff, which explains why she was there the day Eric saw her, but not around when you two went back.' Bex glanced at me to check how I was taking it, picked up a sheet to fold, and went on with her story.

'And the reason why this Eliza-woman was temporary? She's part of some pilot scheme, is what Mark said. A new government thing apparently, where they have trainees working in different museums and galleries. Getting experience of more than one place and finding out how everything works.'

'So she's not there any more?' Bex shook her head.

'She was just there for a couple of weeks, and from what Mark said she won't be back again.'

'So...we can't find her?' I didn't know if I was

pleased or sorry about that. Maybe now Eric had calmed down, we didn't need to keep going right to the bitter end. Bex shook her head again, which could have meant, *No, we can't find her*, but it turned out that she meant, *Yes, we can*. When I thought it was a 'no' I felt a rush of relief as well as disappointment, and when I realised it was actually a 'yes' I felt a rush of fear, but I was excited, too. *Go figure*, is what Susie would say.

'No, we probably *can* find her if we keep looking,' Bex explained. 'But we don't know for sure exactly where she'll be next, because this training scheme takes you off anywhere. And Mark didn't know her surname. Not that it's surprising, not knowing that,' Bex added. 'No one knows anyone's surname any more; might as well not have them! But he – Mark, that is – thinks she was off to do a stint at a place down on the South Bank.'

I felt curious. 'How did you get Mark to tell you all that?' I asked. It all sounded like it had been surprisingly easy – like how it is in a movie, not how it is in real life. Bex grinned mischievously.

'I spun him a line. I told him my flatmate had seen this woman in the shop and fallen for her in a major way. Love at first sight, all that. I told Mark that my flatmate chatted her up and really liked her, and he'd gone back in with a bunch of flowers to ask her out on a date – and she wasn't there! He was crushed, the flatmate, so he'd asked me to find out where she'd gone, so that he could turn up with flowers at the new place, instead.' Bex grinned at me again. 'I was good!' she said. 'Really convincing. Mark was gripped by the whole thing. I reckon he's a bit of a romantic; he really went for the flower idea.'

She'd finished the sheets, so now we only had the duvet covers left to fold. 'So anyway,' she continued, 'we can take this another step forward if you still want to. You can go down to the South Bank with Eric and look around for her, and how about I come with you this time? Unless you think I'll be in the way? It might be a good idea to have a bit of company, just in case. I think your dad might feel easier about it if I tagged along.'

I thought about that while we finished folding and Bex sorted another load into the washing machine. I thought I'd be OK with the whole thing – taking it another step forward sounded almost sensible, until you remembered what it was actually all about. Still...

'But whereabouts on the South Bank?' I asked her. 'Where would we start? It's a big place, you know, and it stretches right along the river from Waterloo Bridge up to Tower Bridge. There's more than one art gallery, for starters, and all those theatres and concert halls and stuff. It'd be hard to cover them all.' And while I was still thinking about the task being way too big, and maybe we couldn't do it after all, Bex dropped her bombshell.

'Oh, didn't I say?' she asked casually, sorting towels. 'Mark had a suggestion about that, after we'd chatted on for a while. He thought Eliza might be doing her next stint in the Poetry Library. She was keen on poetry, he told me, so she was looking forward to going there.'

I stared at Bex in horror. Then I slid down to the floor of the laundry room, and burst into tears.

12

Bex dropped the towels and sat beside me on the floor. She put her arm round my shoulders and stroked my hand, and for ages she didn't say anything or ask me why I was crying, which was just as well; I couldn't have answered. It was like a dam bursting. The tears rushed down and soaked my T-shirt, my eyes swelled up and the muscles in my chin went all twisty. I kept trying to calm myself down. I'd take a breath to gulp back the tears, but every time a new wave of miserableness washed over me and it all started up again. It was awful.

Bex just sat there making soothing noises, and after a while my actual sobbing eased off, and I got to the shivery stage, which is where you notice that your nose is running and your ears hurt, and you start to feel embarrassed. I rubbed at my face, trying to clean up a bit, and Bex got up to pass me some wet kitchen towel, which helped. Then she sat down again for more hand-patting. I felt wrung out, but I'd more or less stopped crying.

'It was the Poetry Library,' I said finally, trying to explain. 'That's what set me off.' My voice had gone croaky with crying, and just hearing it like that reminded me how I'd been right after Mum died.

'Oh, Lizzie, darling, I am *so* sorry,' Bex said softly. 'I didn't know. I suppose if I'd thought about it...but no one's mentioned the library to me. No one even said that your mum was keen on poetry, although now I think of it, I should have guessed, what with that spell you do for Eric, and looking for fox poems, and I know you write poems yourself. And there's that one you wrote with your mum, isn't there? Framed on your wall – I've seen it hundreds of times.' Bex shifted uncomfortably on the floor. 'I feel stupid!' she added. 'I'm really gutted; it was a dreadful thing to do to you.'

I reached over and patted her hand, which was easier than talking right then, and I didn't want her to feel upset. It wasn't her fault; none of this was. Bex shifted again, and then put her arm back around me.

'Did your mum go to the Poetry Library, then?' she asked. But Mum hadn't, not so far as I knew, and I told Bex that.

'No, it was the poetry, not the actual place,' I explained. 'I've never even been to it myself; I just know it's there. Inside the Festival Hall. But it – it just *sounded* like Mum. She – she loved poetry.' When I said that I almost started crying all over again, but I took some slow breaths and the crying went back underground.

Bex squeezed my shoulder. 'I'm really sorry, love. All I was thinking of was finding a good way to tell you about tracking this woman down. I never thought...' Her voice trailed off, but suddenly I wanted to talk to her about it all.

'It's because in my head, I know this person can't *really* be Mum.' I looked at Bex and she nodded. 'But every time I feel even halfway confident that it isn't Mum, something else happens to make me think it *is* her, after all. Or that it *could* be her, even though know it can't be. And then – oh, I don't know how to explain how I feel. So confused and up in the air all the time, and I just hate, hate, HATE it.'

'Because you know she can't come back, and you wish she could?' suggested Bex gently, but I shook my head.

'Because it makes me feel so jumpy and scared. Because I wonder if everything I remember is a lie. And because it's another thing that Eric doesn't know about, and he won't understand why he doesn't, and I don't know how to help him with that. And when I do try to help it goes wrong and I have to start all over again. That's why.' Which was about as clear as mud, and even though Bex nodded I thought she was just being supportive, and that she couldn't really understand what I was talking about. And what I'd said wasn't even the most important part of the truth. I thought I really wanted to tell Bex, but when it came to it, I couldn't, even though what Bex had suggested was closer to the truth than I'd admitted.

I'd learned how to be OK after Mum died. It had taken ages, because I hadn't wanted to learn it; all I wanted, after she died, was for it not to be true and for Mum to come back again, because I missed her so much. But I'd got there in the end, and now I didn't have the faintest clue how I'd be if it turned out that, after all that, she was still around. You might think I'd be singing and dancing at the very idea, but that wasn't it at all. I wasn't about to turn cartwheels and hang out flags and cheer, if it turned out that she *was* the person Eric saw. Not having Mum in my life was like a scar on my heart. And thinking that she might not be dead at all – it was like that scar opening up and hurting all over again.

Because if she wasn't dead, where had she been?

Why would she have left us? And why would Dad have said she was dead if she wasn't? Because how could it be a good thing to think that everything you knew about someone could be turned upside down like that? It all felt so wrong.

And there was a secret reason, too. One I've never told anyone before: not Dad, not Susie. No one, ever.

In a way, I've always felt that Mum was still with me. It's my version of Eric talking out loud to her and to the memory box, I suppose, except that my way's totally private. Sometimes I talk to Mum in my thoughts, like I said before, but what started to happen right after I lost her is that she began to say things to me inside my head. Not words exactly, which is why it's so hard to explain. It's never been out loud or in speech; it was more a feeling that turned into words, and I knew it was Mum doing it.

The feelings said things to me like, *You'll be fine, Lizzie love.* Or, *I love you, take care of yourself.* I got a definite idea that I was being watched over, which was a big comfort, and I treasured it. It used to happen a lot, and then not so much. But since Eric said he saw Mum in the gift shop, it hasn't happened at all.

And now I thought: *If Mum's not dead, then she'll never be inside my head saying those things again, and looking out for me*. And that would probably mean that I'd lost her for ever.

I'd calmed down by the time Eric and Dad came back from the park. There was no danger that I'd start sobbing again any time soon, which was a relief. I wouldn't want to cry like that in front of Eric because he'd be scared. But I felt like a steamroller had squashed me flat, and I thought they'd notice that I was quieter than usual, but as it turned out they didn't see anything was different about me. Eric bounced around the flat like he was riding a pogo stick; he was over the moon with excitement because he'd been chosen for the football team, and so had Sim, which put the icing on Eric's cake.

He told me in a confidential tone that Sim was better at passing balls than he was, so Sim was going to be a sweeper. I'd never heard of a sweeper in football, but that's what he said. Mind you, he also said that he – Eric – was better at ducking and weaving and running than Sim was, so he was going to be an outback! It turned out he'd meant to say *fullback*, and Bex teased him about saying outback by mistake. She asked him if he and Sim were going to sweep the Australian outback together. I watched Eric deciding not to sulk about being teased, which usually sets him off. There was just a moment when I thought he'd make a fuss about it, but then he shrugged and grinned back at Bex. It was a relief; I'd had enough dramas.

Bex kept being particularly kind to me. She even stayed after dinner long enough to put me to bed, which I don't remember her doing before. I know I'm really too old for that, but I loved being babied for a change. And before she put out my light she gave me a kiss and another big hug. She said, 'I'll sort it, my lovely Lizzie. No more worrying, OK?' And I couldn't make her a promise on the worrying front, because worrying is part of my nature and it's a hard habit to break once you're in the groove, but I went to sleep telling myself I'd really try to cut back on worries once all this was over.

But the next morning, though, all my promises and good resolutions went straight out the window. Because the next thing I did was, I completely lost it with Dad.

I knew Bex must have told him about me being upset. I don't know what she said and frankly I'd rather not know, because I feel self-conscious about all the sobbing I did, and I have to hope she didn't say how long it lasted. But I could see Dad knew something had happened because he was extra nice to me at breakfast. And then we cleared the breakfast things away together because Eric was tidying his room. Dad had looked at it before breakfast and said it looked like a pigsty, and Eric wasn't to come out until everything was in apple-pie order. Eric didn't like that at all but he didn't argue, which was another definite improvement. So I still felt fine until Dad turned to me and said, 'You know you can tell me anything, Lizzie? Anything at all?'

Before all the troubles, if he'd said that to me, I'd have thought it was sweet of him. But when he came out with it that day all I could think about was what had been going on, and how I *knew* he was keeping things from me. It was like what people say about a red rag and a bull – I was fine one moment and furious the next: from nought to ninety in a couple of seconds.

I stared at him in disbelief, my heart pounding and my stomach churning. And then I said, 'Oh, please! Just like how *you* tell me *everything*, right?'

Dad stared back at me, absolutely amazed. I thought maybe he hadn't taken in what I'd said, how rude I'd been – or even that he might ignore it, which would be even worse. And by then I was shaking with anger and frustration, and I dropped the plates into the sink with a clatter.

'You're treating me like a child!' I shouted in his

face. 'I might not be a difficult teenager yet but I have feelings, and I have opinions, and I know you're not telling me things *right now*!'

'Lizzie...' Dad started to say something but he ran out of steam. He just stood there holding a tea towel and staring at me like he'd never seen me before. And of course he hadn't seen me like this before – I'd never shouted at him in my whole life.

'This is a mess!' I went on shouting. I threw some spoons into the sink after the plates, and enjoyed the extra noise they made. 'It's a complete mess, and Eric's in a tangle, and you're not doing anything to help him! You say you are, but you're *not*! You'd rather ignore it! You're worrying about it inside your head, but you're not doing anything to help Eric or me. You're just pretending! Trying to make out like it'll be OK on its own! Well, you know what, Dad? It won't be! It's getting worse, not better!'

Dad opened his mouth again but I didn't give him a chance, I just ran him down with more words of my own before he could say any.

'And you know what else?' I shouted. 'If we're *really* Just Us Three together, all-for-one-and-one-for-all – what a joke! – we should be *trusting* each other, and *helping* each other, not closing our eyes and hoping it'll all go away!'

There was a bit of a silence then, because I'd run out of shouting. I hadn't known I was going to say it all, but I definitely felt better for it. I didn't know what Dad would do, but he didn't shout back at me, or even disagree or try to defend himself. He stood there for a bit after I'd finished shouting, looking shocked. But then he put down the tea towel and sort of squared his shoulders a bit, and gave a little nod.

'Fair enough, Lizzie,' he said. 'I think that's – fair enough.' Then he grinned weakly, and muttered something about it being no more than he deserved. He gave me a cautious pat on the shoulder, like he thought I might blow up all over again if he wasn't careful. And I think he was going to have another try at answering me, but then we heard Bex's key in the door, and Eric came out and said his room looked like a new pin and who was going to give him a star for it, and the moment passed. After that, he left for work.

It took me longer than it should have to work out what he meant about it being what he deserved. When I finally did, though, it shook me up all over again. He meant that he *had* lied to me! He meant there *was* something he wasn't telling me!

13

Nothing really happened for the next few days. I thought Dad would want to sit down and talk, but he didn't – although he said a couple of strange things that I didn't get. Like, the next night when I went to bed, he said, 'I'm on the case, Lizzie,' and the next morning when Eric was in the bathroom Dad leaned over the breakfast table and muttered, 'I'm sorting this out now, I promise,' like it was a secret. But I didn't want any more secrets.

Before all this started, Dad telling me the truth was never something I worried about. I just always assumed that he did, like I assumed he meant everything for the best. I didn't like that being different now, but it was, and I felt awkward with him. On the surface, Dad was still just the Dad I knew – rushing around with his hair pulled into a tangle and his eyebrows shooting up, trying to make sure everything was going smoothly in our lives. But now I would look at him, and the thought, *Is he keeping something from me about Mum?* just kept popping back into my mind, and a wave of fed-up-ness would wash over me again. And after I thought it I felt even more awkward with him, of course, although at least some things were clearer now. I mean, look how he was with Eric; trying to pretend nothing was really wrong about him seeing Mum in the Natural History Museum gift shop. *Of course there was something wrong!*

I saw that now, but when it came down to it I wasn't much better at dealing with it than Dad, which made me wonder if Just Us Three was the best idea in the world. When I needed Bex to help, she did, and you can think, *That was lucky*, or you can think, *That shows you need people in your life to say different things to you*. So I had to wonder if it would be better if there were more of us. And once I'd started wondering about that I couldn't stop, and it reminded me to wonder why we don't have any relations at all. Having no uncles and aunts is one thing, and if your parents didn't have any brothers and sisters, that would be why. But parents must have had *their* parents, mustn't they? And I don't ever remember hearing about them, either from Mum's side or from Dad's.

I had asked Dad about grandparents once, and he laughed and said, 'What? Isn't Mrs Oliver enough for you?' It's true that she acts rather like a granny with Eric and me. But afterwards I realised: *That wasn't a straight answer!* Dad did once say that his parents died years ago, but that's all. And he never said anything about Mum's, not even if they were still around. I don't think Mum talked about them either, although it's hard to be sure about that. I wouldn't necessarily remember if she had.

We had all those photos of Mum and lots of Just Us Three, but there weren't any of our relatives or ancestors. Not one. Wasn't that a bit odd as well? It bothered me enough to ask Bex for her opinion, which shows how things were between me and Dad. I didn't ask him again. If you know you can't expect a straight answer, it's hard to shake off that feeling of resentment.

Bex said she didn't think it was all that unusual, especially not to have grandparents around. She never knew her mother's parents because they lived on the other side of Australia when she was growing up, and they died before she could finally catch up with them.

'But look on the bright side, Lizzie,' she added. 'You mightn't like them if you had them, and if you have 'em you can't get rid of 'em; they're yours for life. If family arrive at your door in the middle of the night you can't shout through the keyhole at them, or turn them away. You have to let them in!'

I tried to imagine a whole heap of secret relatives turning up on our doorstep all together, and needing to be put up on lilos on the living-room floor. I thought it might be fun.

And when I asked Bex about photos and why we didn't have any of our relatives, she pointed out that people don't keep photo albums so much these days. 'Except for baby books,' I added, but she's right. Even Dad doesn't print out photos from his camera unless it's for something special. Mum and Dad did keep baby books for me and for Eric, though; we've still got them. Eric loves looking through his. I admit it's fascinating to see what you looked like as a baby.

So it could have all been something and nothing, which is what Mrs Oliver says when things are up in the air and no one knows what's going to happen.

But when Bex suddenly announced that it was all arranged, and she was coming down to the South Bank with me and Eric to visit the Poetry Library, I was completely and majorly up for it.

'I've talked to your dad again,' she said. 'He sees it needs sorting, so don't worry about that. He said

I should go for it, and that he'll do what he has to, as well.'

Yeah, right, is what I thought about Dad's comment, but I didn't say that to Bex. She was still keen to come with us; I suspect she thought I'd object, but I actually didn't mind. I knew I *had* to go, but I probably don't have to say that I wasn't exactly looking forward to it. Having Bex's company was fine by me, especially in case Eric reverted to his old tantrum tricks.

I was inclined not to tell Eric why we were going to the Poetry Library. After all, we might have been going there anyway, like we'd go to a museum. I even wondered if I should go by myself first, and if there actually was a woman in the library who looked like Mum, then OK, we'd take Eric to look at her. But Bex said it'd be better to go just once and get it over with – and then I realised that keeping the real reason from Eric would be like Dad keeping whatever he was keeping from me. And I wanted to be straight with Eric, even though I dreaded getting him all stirred up again.

When I did tell him, it turned out I'd been worrying for nothing! I could have saved myself a whole lot of grief if I'd told him straight away. He was pleased and a bit excited, but he didn't start behaving badly all over again, or talking out loud to invisible people: nothing like that. He just asked lots of questions to get the trip sorted out in his head – like exactly where the library was, and how would we get there, and could he take his scooter down to the South Bank.

I didn't ask Bex exactly what she'd told Dad, or if he knew about her going to the Natural History Museum and what Mark had told her. Bex did say that she'd 'brought Dad up to date', whatever that meant. I was ready to clamp my hands over my ears and sing 'la la la' until she'd finished explaining it to me, but she saw from my expression that I didn't want the details, and she didn't give me any. I didn't even ask her if Dad knew we were all going down to the Festival Hall together. I just assumed it was all OK, unless and until someone told me it wasn't.

So I admit I was a bit of a coward about everything that week. I didn't actually want to open a can of worms myself, like people say about looking for trouble. I didn't want a whole can of secret worms opened and slithering around my life. I wanted to ignore them a while longer, so that's what I did. You can do that successfully, too, although not for ever. But I decided I didn't have to do it for ever – just for a couple more days.

The only thing left to figure out was when to go down to the South Bank. We settled on the next

Saturday afternoon, but then Bex suddenly found out she had an extra reflexology class that day. I looked on the website and saw the Poetry Library stayed open until eight o'clock at night during the week. So I suggested the three of us could go down after school, one day in the week.

'Sounds like a plan!' Bex agreed. So that's what we did.

We got down there just after five o'clock on the Wednesday afternoon, and when we walked through from the tube station I had a bit of a surprise. There were hundreds of people on the South Bank, walking along the river and looking in the shops, or sitting outside the cafés. It was kind of nice in a way, all those people having a good time, and it was really buzzy, as Bex pointed out. But my heart sank when I saw just how many people there were, even on a weekday afternoon. Trying to track down one person in a big crowd would be hard.

I felt less worried, though, once we got inside the Festival Hall. There was hardly anyone in the foyer – you could see from the back of the building, which is where we came in, right through to the front on the river side. And I realised it would be even quieter by the time we got up to the Poetry Library. I mean, I like poetry, but how many other people feel that way? It's not like a pop concert; it's more of a minority entertainment.

So we headed for the stairs that take you up to the Poetry Library, and despite our weird situation, I was actually looking forward to it. Not to the not-Mum bit, of course, but to the library itself. I'd found out you can join it for free and take out books, and although it would be quite a distance to lug books home and back from the South Bank, I planned to give it a try. So I was thinking about that and not so much about the real reason for us being there, when suddenly Eric said, 'Look!'

His voice sounded insistent: it wasn't a *Look, there's a juggler!* voice; more of a *Look, there's something I'm worried about!* voice. My heart gave a thump of fear, and I swung around to see what he was pointing at.

'Look! Over there!' Eric said, even louder. His voice was super-urgent now, and he was staring across the foyer at the back doors: the big glass ones out to the terrace that looks over the river. He pointed, but I still couldn't see anything – or anyone – special. There were quite a few people going in and out. Bex bent down and took his shoulder.

'Where, Eric? Show me!' she said, but he wasn't waiting any longer.

'It's her!' he hissed, shaking off Bex's hand. 'It's

Mum again!' And he took off. I said before that Eric's fast, but I never knew just how fast – he was across the foyer and pulling desperately at the big glass doors before I could even think of stopping him, let alone try to do it.

'Eric! Wait!' That was Bex, off after him. She was frantic not to lose sight of him, especially if he got outside without us. I didn't waste my breath calling out as well, I just took off as fast as I could, which was about as good as Bex but nowhere near as fast as Eric.

People actually swerved aside as Bex and I hurtled across the foyer, and I thought we'd be bound to catch Eric up at the doors. But then someone opened them from the outside, and he ducked through them and disappeared outside onto the terrace. I got to the doors and wrenched at them, but they're incredibly heavy and I couldn't seem to shift them at all. I tried pulling instead of pushing, but I just couldn't do it. I felt totally panicked, because right then I'd had a new and terrible thought. *What if this mystery woman steals Eric?*

'Here, let me,' panted Bex, taking over. And as soon as she'd heaved the doors open far enough I dashed to the edge of the terrace, looking every which way. But I couldn't see Eric anywhere, and by then, despite all my stamina training, I also had a slight stitch in my side. So then I was standing on the terrace, clutching my waist and trying to peer around at Eric-height at the same time. Bex could see further than me because she's taller, and when she arrived a few seconds later she jumped up and down on the spot, turning from side to side as she did so to get a good view all around. I'd have got the giggles if I hadn't been so worried about losing Eric. She did look funny: like a crazy dog jumping for a biscuit.

'There, I think!' she called, pointing down to the broad pavement beside the river. 'Look! Isn't that him?' And she was off again, across the terrace and down the steps to the river-front. I didn't stop to check where she'd pointed in case I lost sight of Bex as well as Eric, which would have been a total disaster. I just ran straight after her, trying to dodge people coming up the steps and saying, 'Sorry... sorry,' all the way down. *Mrs Oliver would be pleased about my manners*, I suddenly thought, and I'd have started giggling about that, if I'd had the time. It's funny how silly things just pop into your mind when you're under pressure.

Bex caught up with Eric in front of the National Film Theatre. He was looking around wildly, and he didn't take much notice of Bex when she grabbed his arm, or of me, either, when I arrived. 'It was her!' he kept saying, still looking around urgently. 'She was heading this way, but when I got here she'd disappeared.'

I stood still, and turned slowly around on the spot, searching the crowds, and Bex tried hopping on the spot again. 'Red hair,' said Eric, calming down a bit now that he had helpers. 'Like yours, only shorter. And a green top.' Bex stopped hopping up and down and tried turning on the spot like me, but in the opposite direction. There were just too many people around. I didn't see how –

'There!' Eric shouted at the top of his voice. 'Mum! Wait!' And then he'd ducked under Bex's arm and was off again, racing along the river walk. I tell you, I was impressed with his speed all over again.

'Oh *no*,' Bex murmured, but we didn't waste time or breath saying things to each other like, *Come on*, or, *Let's follow him*. We just did it.

Eric was running towards Waterloo Bridge and shouting at the top of his voice, 'Mu-uu-m! Wait!'

Everyone was skipping out of his way, and he was dodging in and out of the crowds like he was doing a slalom. Bex and I hurtled after him as quickly as we could, which wasn't as quick as Eric, and we were dodging in and out and saying, 'Sorry...sorry... sorry...' again. I kept trying to look ahead of Eric as well as keep track of him, because I wanted to get a look at this woman – the not-Mum mystery person who'd caused us so much trouble.

And that's when I saw – not Mum, and not not-Mum either. I saw *Dad*! I couldn't believe it at first, but it truly was him. He was up on Waterloo Bridge, peering through the railings and looking around at the crowds. He hadn't spotted any of us, but I was so shocked to see him there I stared at him for too long, and stopped looking where I was going. I stumbled over a paving stone and almost fell, and by the time I'd recovered and looked back at where Dad had been, he wasn't there any more.

He should be at work! was my first thought. And the next one was, *But what's he doing here? And where's he gone now? And...* And then I completely forgot about Dad, because suddenly there was a gap in the crowd right in front of me.

And there was Eric, with not-Mum beside him. Eric was pulling at her arm, looking up at her and holding out the dragon chain. And not-Mum crouched down beside him looking amazed and surprised, and majorly confused. So what I saw was this woman staring at the dragon chain, and then looking back at Eric, and fingering the chain like it was the most astonishing thing she'd ever seen.

She definitely wasn't Mum.

That was my first thought. But then she saw Eric looking back at me and so she turned around and looked straight at me, too. And then, well, she kind of rocked back on her heels, and gasped out loud. I couldn't hear the gasp, but I saw her do it. And I gasped, too.

Because OK, it *wasn't* Mum, and from the back she hadn't looked all that much like her. *Same colour hair*, is all I'd thought at first. But from the front? Well, that was different. Like Mum in a mirror – well, no, not that much like her really; but still, a *lot* like her. And all of those thoughts tumbled around in my brain, and swirled and bumped into each other, and I felt dizzy and sick. I almost thought I might faint, which I never have done, but then Bex arrived panting beside me, and put her arm around me and held me tight. I'd never been so glad to see anyone in my whole life but I didn't say anything to her. I didn't even look at her. I just kept looking at Eric and the mystery woman.

As soon as I saw not-Mum I didn't want to call her that any more. I knew she had a real name and I knew what her name must be, but I didn't want to use it. So at that stage I just thought of her as Her. I grabbed Bex's hand and squeezed it quickly, to say thank you. Then I let go and walked towards Eric and Her.

I got to within about a metre and then stopped again, but I didn't take my eyes off Her. And she kept looking at me too, and then she said hesitantly, 'Eliza, right?' and stretched out a hand to me. I nodded, and took another step forwards. I wasn't thinking about what was going on; I was just doing each thing one after another, like I was in a trance. And I couldn't stop staring at Her because she looked so like Mum, but at the same time she absolutely *wasn't* Mum.

It was like staring at a picture you might have put together inside your head, and suddenly it had come to life and it was talking to you. She put out a cautious hand and touched my hair very gently, like she wanted to check it was real. I'd have liked to do the same thing to her hair, because it was so like Mum's, but I didn't dare. Not then. But still, I couldn't stop looking.

And the next time I noticed anything else around me Dad was there too, and Bex had stepped forward and grabbed Eric's hand like she'd never let go again. When Dad put his arm around me I saw he was crying, and then I realised I was, too. And through his tears Dad croaked something like, 'Too late, Ellie!' And the ex-mystery woman was crying as well, and she sobbed back at him, 'Not too late at all, Dave! Never too late!' And then she was hugging the bits of Eric that Bex would let go of, and reaching out to me again, and then letting Eric and me go and fumbling around in her handbag. And when she brought her hand out of the bag and opened it, there in her palm was the Saint George half of Eric's dragon chain.

Eric looked at it, and then back at her, like he wasn't in the least surprised. Like he'd known this would happen all along; like it was the only thing that mattered. I was surprised, but by then I wasn't so shocked any more. And by then, well, I'd sort of guessed the truth, and I bet you've probably guessed as well. But it took a whole lot longer than that to sort everything out.

14

The first thing I have to admit now is that it took me ages to stop being angry with Dad. But when I found out what he'd been through, I could see he hadn't had an easy time. In fact, it turned out that Dad had been carrying around a secret sorrow just about for ever, which made me feel sad for him, and that rubbed out a lot of my anger. I didn't even feel cross that he'd never mentioned the secret sorrow, because I could see why he wouldn't have done. Secrets like that are private for the person who has them. It's only when other people are involved that you have to say them out loud. And Dad thought – well, anyway, I'll try to put his story in the right order, because in the end, he explained just about everything.

The story started with Mum's family taking against

him from the very start, and I was so surprised about that, I stopped minding so much about what had happened to me. They took against *Dad*? Why ever should they? You won't know because of not having met him, but he is super-respectable, my Dad. He wears a tie to the office and he always works hard, and almost never swears in front of us. He nags us about saying please and thank you and being generally well behaved, and sitting at the table when we eat meals. I'd have thought you can't get much more respectable than Dad, and I told him that. He was rather pleased – probably because I hadn't said anything nice to him for days and days by then – but he insisted it was true. The whole of Mum's family thought he wasn't good enough for their Alice.

So I asked him if he'd been – oh, I don't know, a tattooed biker or a druggie or something when he was going out with Mum, which might explain why they thought that. But he stared at me like I was crazy, and said stiffly, 'No of course not; I was a management trainee when I met your mother.' And I don't imagine you can't get much more obviously respectable than that, so it's still a mystery to me.

'It got worse than just not liking me,' he went on. 'They actually stopped talking to your mum when we got engaged. They thought she'd get such a fright she'd drop me and run back home, but you couldn't bully Alice like that, and it didn't work. They never forgave her for choosing me over them, though. Her sister Ellie was the only one who came to our wedding, and she didn't exactly come with a glad heart. In fact she stood there with a face like thunder, and then rushed off again straight after the ceremony.' He paused, remembering, and took a breath. 'Your mum was very hurt,' he added softly.

'After that we never saw much more of them,' Dad went on. 'Not even her sister, and they'd been very close growing up. No birthday cards, no Christmas cards, nothing. Alice tried to get in touch from time to time – when you were born, for instance; I know she wrote then, and again with Eric. But they pushed her away or ignored her, every single time.'

'But her sister...?' I'd always thought sisters stuck together.

'Your new Auntie Ellie?' Dad said, with a little smile. 'Well, like I said, Alice and Eliza were very close when they were growing up. They even looked alike when they were girls – they weren't twins, but they pretended they were, and what's more, people believed them! So your mum was very upset when they split up over me. She named you after her

156

sister, you know. I think she hoped it would make a difference, and Ellie did come to see us a couple of times when you were tiny. But after that we never heard from her again, and Alice got hurt all over again. I was very angry about that – it was so unfair.'

'So when Mum died...' I prompted.

'So when she died, I decided I'd had enough of them. I never said we were moving, or where we were going: I didn't want them in our lives – especially not in your lives. You and Eric, you'd had enough sorrow and upsets by then, and I said to myself, *they don't deserve you two*.'

'And then Eric saw Auntie Ellie in the gift shop,' I added. Dad nodded.

'I didn't know it was her, then,' he said. 'I didn't think of her when it happened. It was only later on, when you told me her name was Eliza, too, that I realised it could actually be her: even that it most probably *was* her. But – well, I didn't want to deal with it.'

There was a bit of a silence, while Dad looked uncomfortable. Then he sighed, and said, 'I know I got that wrong, Lizzie. And I know it didn't help the situation, me burying my head in the sand. But give me some credit, at least, for hearing your wake-up call.'

'You mean, when I lost it and shouted at you?'

157

I asked. Dad nodded and looked awkward again.

'That's when I knew I had to sort it out. And I know! *I know!* It took me a long time to get there – *way* too long. Guilty as charged, Lizzie.' He looked so miserable I felt less annoyed, but I was still very curious.

'But what actually changed your mind?' I asked. 'Was it really just me?'

Dad took a deep breath, and let it out again slowly. And then he said, 'Let me put it this way: with you two, being a single parent and working all the hours... Well, you can get stuck in a rut. I got into one, anyway. An automatic-pilot sort of thing.' He ticked off imaginary ideas on his fingers. '*A problem with Eric?* Right: the solution's to ignore the drama, and he'll calm down again. *A problem with Lizzie?* Right: the solution's easy, because there never is a problem with Lizzie...' He grinned at me. 'And I was wrong on both counts! You can't put people into boxes like that. I didn't see that's what I was doing, but I did. And if I've learned anything from this, it's that you two deserve better than that from me.' And then he paused and swallowed, like the next thing was extra-hard to say.

'One more thing for me to say sorry to you about, Lizzie. I shouldn't have stopped you going to your mother's funeral.'

I was surprised by that, because I didn't have a bad memory about it; I didn't even remember wanting to go to the funeral. But maybe Dad was right.

And then he was off again with his next idea, which turned out to be looking for things the two of us could do together. A Just-Us-Two plan of action. I was majorly pleased to have him suggest that, but we had a bit of trouble working out the right thing to start us off until Dad looked sheepish and said, 'What about databases?' I couldn't help laughing – databases don't sound like a father–daughter kind of thing, even though I know it's his IT speciality. But he explained that I could have found the fox poems for Eric if I'd used a database – like the ones they have at the Poetry Library, as it happens. I was touched he'd thought it all through, especially because of Mum and poetry, so I gave him a hug and we both cried a little bit, and after that I felt tons better.

By then, of course, I knew that not-Mum (ex-mystery woman; Her) was really Ellie – Eliza, Mum's long-lost sister. The one Eric saw in the Natural History Museum, and then again on the South Bank. But the funniest-peculiar thing about the whole South Bank experience was that, when Eric spotted her, she was actually on her way to a coffee bar to meet Dad! Because by then *he'd* tracked her down; he'd rung her at the Poetry Library – completely out of the blue, as far as she knew – and asked her to meet him for coffee. He was planning to put her in the picture, and tell her everything that had happened – about Eric seeing her and thinking she was Mum, and then us going back to the Natural History Museum to look at her again, only to find she'd left.

And now that we were going to look again, he'd wanted to agree a plan with her about what to do when we found her.

Dad didn't know we were down on the South Bank that day and heading for the Poetry Library ourselves, because Bex had planned on the Saturday.

When Dad explained that part I suddenly understood why he'd said 'Too late!' to Aunt Ellie in that dramatic way when he'd arrived. It was because he'd wanted to talk to her *before* she met me and Eric, not wait until after he found us all together in a heap on the pavement.

Bex was right: Dad had been trying to do right by us. Just a bit late. But you have to hope that, like Auntie Ellie said, it's never too late to say sorry and to start all over again.

I'd never guessed that Mum and her sister shared

the Saint George and the Dragon medallion. Well, I couldn't have guessed, could I? Mum never told me, and Dad didn't say. I'll ask Aunt Ellie about it some time, because I wonder if they broke it on purpose so that each of them could have a bit. But Eric's got both halves now, anyway, and he's over the moon with satisfaction.

One bit of Dad's story was definitely funny-ha-ha instead of funny-peculiar, though he still doesn't know why. It was when he was talking to me and Eric about what had happened, and Bex was there too, like she often is, because she's still a kind of honorary one-for-all-er, in my opinion.

Dad explained that when he'd realised he had to find Aunt Ellie, he'd started by going to the Natural History Museum. He said the guy he spoke to there was helpful, and recognised the description that Dad gave, as well – and of course, Dad could mention Ellie's name. 'But I tell you what was weird,' Dad added, frowning. 'This guy at the museum? He asked me where the bunch of flowers was, and he kind of grinned knowingly, and waggled his eyebrows at me. What that was all about, I'll never understand.'

And he didn't understand why Bex and I glanced at each other in delight, and then burst out laughing.

*

When I told Susie the whole story, she said it sounded exactly like something off the telly. Then she grinned, and said it was more *X-Files* than *Desperate Housewives*. I had to laugh. And it is weird, I grant her that, but probably no weirder than the secrets that lots of families keep hidden away.

Dad's still giving me the credit. He claims that it was what I'd said to him that finally tipped the balance, and that's when he realised where he'd gone wrong. He says he'll always be grateful to me for putting the one-for-all-ers back on track, which is actually majorly generous of him.

Bex says I shouldn't be too hard on him. She said all parents get some things wrong; they can't help it, they're only human. 'Everyone makes mistakes,' she said. 'What matters is what you do to put them right: that's what counts.' And she also said I should look on the bright side, because now I have an aunt. I'd been going on about wanting more relatives, and hey presto! Now I had one.

Eric's been the biggest surprise. He's so relaxed about how it all turned out, and he doesn't seem like the same person he was just a little while ago. But then, he probably isn't the same. I know I'm not. He just says he always knew he could find the other half of the dragon chain, and now he had, and he'd also found us an aunt we never knew about, so everyone believed him now, didn't they? He's very matter-of-fact about Aunt Ellie, too. I think he likes her because he found her, so he thinks she's his property.

And his fox project is over, and the biscuits went down well in the presentation. But the biggest success was when he sang the fox song right through to the whole class, and remembered all the words. And he came home that day fizzing with pleasure and said, 'They honestly liked me, Lizzie!' in a way that made me realise he probably hadn't fitted in well at school before, and now he did. So he's on a roll, with Sim, and his football, and everything, and I can stop worrying about him for a while.

But what Eric's most interested in now is Mum. He's accepted she isn't around and she won't ever be, but he still wants to tell her things – just in a different way. So he and I have decided to write a letter to Mum, and tell her everything that happened, because it's a good story and, like Eric said, she'll want to know that something's improved in our lives. We're going to tell her the whole background, about how Ellie still had her half of the dragon chain and carried it in her purse everywhere she went. And that now, instead of the broken medallion, Auntie Ellie carries a photo of Eric and me around in her handbag!

And we'll tell her that Aunt Ellie's trying to make her peace with Dad. I was worried about that because of the sorrow that Ellie caused Mum, but she's trying to put things right and she's family. And like Bex says, families are for ever, even if some of them don't realise it at the time. As for me, I'd rather have Bex, but I'll give Auntie Ellie a fair chance like I should do. We'll see more of her now that she's in London, but Dad says it's early days, and he wants to take it slowly.

'Mum won't be surprised about that if you put it in your letter,' he said. 'She always knew I had a cautious nature.' I almost asked him if he wanted to write a letter to her like we were doing, before I realised that for all I know, he already does that. And when Eric and I have finished our letter, and when Eric's drawn pictures to go with it, we'll put it all in Eric's memory box and close the lid.

Bex is right, there *is* a bright side to it all, and I know what it is. I know now that I'll never lose Mum. I thought I'd lost her, but I've found her again. She's in my heart for ever, and in Eric's too, and Dad's: even in Aunt Ellie's. We all remember different bits of her, or in Eric's case we've made them up instead, but by now even the made-up bits are a true part of Mum. I thought I knew everything about her, but I absolutely didn't, and no one else knew everything about her, either. But what we have is enough to go on with, now.

Note from the Author

The three lines of poetry on page 6 are from 'Mazeppa' by George Gordon, Lord Byron.

'Wynken, Blynken and Nod', also quoted on page 6, is a nursery rhyme by Eugene Field.

The two poems about foxes mentioned on page 42 are 'The Thought-Fox' by Ted Hughes, and 'The Three Foxes' by A. A. Milne.

The 7-line quotation on page 44 is from 'A Spell for Sleeping' by Alistair Reid.

The song 'The Fox', quoted on page 62, is a traditional folk song.

The poem Dad tries to remember on page 72 and 73 is 'If' by Rudyard Kipling.

More fantastic novels by
Belinda Hollyer...

ISBN 978 1 84616 690 7 £5.99

*Mini loves her older sister Kate – she means
the world to her.*

So when Kate disappears without a trace, Mini is devastated.
But she's determined to find her sister, and an unsuspected
secret is her first clue to tracking Kate down...and fixing her
broken family.

More fantastic novels by
Belinda Hollyer...

ISBN 978 1 84362 943 6 £5.99

Jessye loves living with her nana, but when her carefree mother
sweeps back into her life, she is forced to grow up and make
some difficult decisions – for secrets lurk beneath the surface
of all their lives...

"A beautiful and moving novel." *Margaret Mahy*

More fantastic novels by Belinda Hollyer...

ISBN 978 1 84362885 9 £4.99

She's not my true sister, she just can't be.

Something strange is going on, and I intend to find out what it is.

When Josie Green becomes a family detective for her school history project, she comes across secrets she wasn't meant to discover. Confused and angry, Josie's determined to unravel the truth – but when she finally succeeds it's more shocking than she ever imagined...

"An up-to-the-minute contemporary novel, warmly told and totally involving." *Jacqueline Wilson*

Turn the page for
more great titles
from Orchard...

More fabulous novels from Orchard

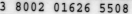